CONTROLLING
DARKNESS

A CONTROL SERIES NOVEL

Anna Edwards

Darkness needs
light.

Anna
Edwards
x

This is a work of fiction. Names, characters, places, and incidents are a product of the author's imagination. Locales and public names are sometimes used for atmospheric purposes. Any resemblance to actual people, living or dead, or to businesses, companies, events, institutions, or locales is completely coincidental.

Warning: This book contains sexually explicit scenes and adult language and may be considered offensive to some readers. This book is for sale to adults only, as defined by the laws of the country in which you made your purchase.

Disclaimer: Please do not try any sexual practice, without the guidance of an experienced practitioner. Neither the publisher nor the author will be responsible for any loss, harm, injury or death resulting from the use of the information contained in this book.

Cover Design by www.CharityHendry.com
Logo Design by Charity Hendry
Editing by Dayna Hart, Hart to Heart Edits
Formatting by Charity Hendry

Controlling Darkness/ Anna Edwards -- 1st ed.
ISBN 978-1546472292

Dedication

To my dear friend, John. You've always been such a help and guiding light in my life. From school work, to university and into adulthood. I cannot thank you enough for your proof reading and ideas that you send me based on my writing. They have furthered my writing to no end. I know that you are having a scary time at the moment but you have always proved to be a stubborn bastard (your words not mine); so I know that you will beat this. Much love to you. x

CONTENTS

CHAPTER ONE

Sonia

"Mummy? Mummy, wake up." The little girl crawled closer to the still body on the floor. "Mummy?" Minutes turned to hours. Nothing changed. Her mummy didn't wake up. Sirens filled her head, and a policeman rushed in.

"Come on, little one. Shall we go find a teddy for you to cuddle?"

"Why won't mummy wake up?"

"She is very tired. The doctors will come and look after her." His anguished face looked to the cold figure on the floor.

"Oh. I will get my toy cat; it is called Mr Whiskers." The little girl took his hand, and as he led her from the kitchen, she called back over her shoulder. "Have a good sleep mummy."

....

Sonia sat up on the bed, sweat drenching the tangled mess of sheets. No, not again.

Why tonight? Tomorrow was the first day of her new job. She'd trained so hard for it. Sonia tried to straighten the sheets and padded into the kitchen to make hot chocolate. Too many memories stirred after that dream.

Why? Why did her stupid subconscious have to remind her now?

"Mummy" echoed through her head.

She had only been seven when she found her mother, twisted and bleeding on the kitchen floor; dead, though she hadn't realised it at the time. Her life changed dramatically that day, it derailed, and she was finally getting it back on track. 'Come on Sonia. You're stronger than this. Don't let him win!

Her hands stopped shaking, and she picked up the hot chocolate and drifted back into the bedroom, and the next thing she knew, her alarm clock was shrilling out to wake her with a jolt.

It hadn't taken Sonia long to dress in a smart suit, grab a breakfast of croissants and a skinny Americano, and travel the short distance across London from her one-bedroom flat in Hackney to the Central London offices of North Enterprises. The massive, shimmering structure loomed up skywards in front of her. Okay. She could do this. She had been through a rigorous training regime and had been selected from candidates she thought far superior. But the man-mountain who told her she had the job seemed to empathise with her past work. She had originally trained for the police but had quickly become jaded with all the bureaucracy. After that, she moved into a branch of the Metropolitan Police's Protection Command for a year, and then transferred to guarding private clientele. She had travelled to lots of places, protected an assortment of people, and enjoyed every minute of it. This was most definitely the career for her.

Sonia was escorted up to the top floor of the building and into the expansive office of Mr James North. Behind him stood the man who had interviewed her, Mr Carter. Mr North stood and held his hand out to her.

"Miss Anderson, a pleasure to meet you. Please take a seat. Matthew has told you of the job specifications?"

Sonia sat on the offered seat, her legs to the side and hands folded neatly in her lap. She so wanted to make the right impression to her new boss at this first meeting.

"He has, Mr North. I am to ensure Miss Jones' safety at all times, but at present, I am to stay back and not allow her to know that she has a bodyguard. Mr Carter will accompany her when you don't need him, and I will report back to him for all instructions. Under no circumstances am I to acknowledge you. I will maintain this cover unless I feel it necessary to break it to protect Miss Jones from either physical or emotional harm."

"Superb!" Mr North looked up at his bodyguard. "I have a meeting, but after that, I will be taking Amy shopping. Matthew, provide Sonia with everything she needs. Please give her the keys to the Lexus." Matthew nodded at Mr North as the latter left the room. He hadn't spoken the entire time she had been in the office.

She had learnt about him during the training phase. He was often silent; it gave him an allure of mystery and power. Sonia had first met him when he had just finished a workout. He was wearing only a pair of shorts, he was toned and muscular in all the right places, and even his shorts looked as if they could barely contain his statuesque thighs. His hair had been messed by the towel he had been drying himself with. Sonia must have looked like one of those cartoon characters whose long tongue rolled out and along the floor when they saw something that sexy. Matthew had given her a pleasant smile and gone into business mode.

"Miss Anderson, I hope you're not prone to daydreaming when on duty."

Matthew's voice broke through her reflections. She bit her tongue and looked guiltily down at the ground.

"Sorry Mr Carter, just a little nervous after meeting Mr North. He is overawing."

Matthew laughed, "Give him a week, and you'll see he is a pussy cat. Miss Jones has the measure of him already."

"Is that why he isn't telling her she has a bodyguard?"

"The relationship between Miss Jones and Mr North is still in the early stages. Mr North understands that he needs protection to ensure his safety, but Miss Jones is independent and somewhat naive. They tend to clash a little as they sort out their differing opinions. I am sure you'll see that this afternoon."

"I think I understand. Miss Jones thinks a bodyguard will

take her independence away, but Mr North knows she'll be a target because of her association with him and his wealth?"

"Not just that. Miss Jones has an unpredictable uncle. Mr North has just shown Miss Jones several things about him she was unaware off. We aren't sure if Mr Jones will try to talk to his niece again. This isn't to happen for any reason. He is a very dangerous man. Do you understand that?"

"Yes, of course. Do you have a photo of him?"

Matthew strode towards a safe, punched in a combination, and pulled some papers out. He also retrieved a gun. He brought them back to the desk and handed Sonia a picture.

"This is Stephen Jones. No criminal convictions but he is suspected of murder, grievous bodily harm, human trafficking, and pimping. He is a nasty piece of work, and recently ordered his own girlfriend have their child beaten from her stomach and joined in himself 'just for fun'."

No wonder Mr North wanted Miss Jones protected from him. "I will make sure he gets nowhere near her."

"Thank you. This is for you as well." He handed her the gun. "You're aware of how to use it?"

"Yes, Sir."

"It is for emergencies only. Here, if you're caught with it, this will give you a reason." He handed her a piece of paper.

"MI5?"

"I used to work for them. Still have contacts."

Sonia hadn't used a gun much in the past for her work, but she had trained with them and had spent a lot of time on the shooting ranges and hostage simulations perfecting her technique. It was a powerful emotion when she was able to hit her targets with one hundred percent accuracy.

"I better show you your car, and then I need to go and collect Miss Jones. I don't think she is looking forward to this shopping trip, but most of her clothes have been ruined, and she needs lots of clothes for the upcoming trip to India. Not that she knows about that yet."

"India?"

"Yes, which reminds me. I will need your passport so that I can sort out the visa for you to come as well. Can you make sure you bring it tomorrow, please?"

"Of course, Mr Carter."

"Mr Carter is my father, Sonia, please call me Matthew."

"Matthew it is, then," Sonia smiled, this job was going to be complex, but she was already relishing the excitement of it. The last man she had protected had been an eighty-year-old ex-banker. He was still in his heyday when local London mobster's wanted to see him destroyed for financing the wrong gang. It had been a pretty boring job, she spent most of her time walking him around in his wheelchair and trying to avoid his wandering hands. No, this job was going to be vastly different. She was certain of that. It was going to be a breath of fresh air and one that got her away from all the fears that she was trying to suppress from her past.

After what seemed like hours of driving around London, they pulled up at the shop on Oxford Street, and Miss Jones actually agreed to get out of the car. They had been to Bond Street and Regent Street, but each time the car pulled away. Mr North and Miss Jones got out of the car and headed into Topshop, the former with a heavy frown on his face. Sonia followed Matthew to park the vehicles. Within minutes they re-joined their already bored-looking boss. Amy had a couple of items in her hand, and James was showing her other things, but every time she looked at the price tag and said no. Sonia was impressed. Sonia had seen plenty of gold diggers. Eventually, however, Miss Jones caved under her boyfriend's pressure, and Matthew stood with his arms piled high with clothing. Sonia tried not to laugh at him as he looked over and rolled his eyes. She ducked behind a mannequin and dug through the pile of jeans as if she were looking for her size.

When Amy went into the changing rooms, Sonia went into the next cubicle. After about an hour and lots of arguments later, they all went back to Knightsbridge and Sonia followed in the Lexus. It was a nice car, and she was beginning to love driving it. It was going to be difficult leaving it to get the tube home.

Sonia went into the car park and waited for Matthew. Eventually, he strolled down into the garage, one hand in the pocket of his tailored suit, and a glass of water with ice and lemon in the other.

"Here, this is for you. You need to make sure you've a bottle of something with you in future. Rookie mistake getting dehydrated on the job, especially in the summer. It slows the reflexes. I should have asked you this morning if you had anything."

Sonia took the glass and drank it down quickly. "Thank you. I normally always bring water. What do you need me to do now?"

"You can take off for the night. He has to cook Miss Jones dinner as punishment for making her spend too much money. So they won't be leaving the house again." The bodyguard laughed as his spoke. His voice was gravelly and reverberated around Sonia's body causing nearly every hair to stand on end. No man had done that to her in a while, in fact, no man had ever done that to her. Men only caused trouble and destroyed lives. She had had no need for one, both for companionship or physically. Her hand and a friendly rabbit were just as good. And for companionship her four-year-old tabby cat, called Mr Whiskers was perfect. Matthew was standing in front of her awaiting an answer. She had drifted off again in thought.

"Sorry. I am not normally so spacey. I was nervous and didn't sleep too well last night."

"No worries, I get it. This probably isn't like any assignment that you've had before. Mr North is slightly intense, but once you get to know him, and he is able to tell Miss Jones about you, I am sure it will be easier."

"Thanks."

"Look I am going to head to the gym. I generally use Mr North's, but I am also a member of one down the road. Do you want to come with me? I can sign you in as a guest."

"Is that okay? Doesn't Mr North need you to protect him here?"

"He has a way of contacting me if he needs me. I am not at his beck and call. That would drive me insane. Inside the house, he is perfectly safe."

"Ok, I would like that. My gym is a bit dodgy but all I can afford. I suspect a Knightsbridge one is the height of luxury by comparison."

Matthew laughed again. "I wouldn't bet on that!"

CHAPTER TWO

Matthew

Matthew hunched over his knee and pulled the twenty-five-kilo weight into a bicep curl. His workout had been somewhat disjointed as he found himself watching Sonia pound out mile after mile on the runner. He couldn't fault her cardio strength. That would definitely come in handy. Matthew was getting too old for that shit. Which reminded him, he needed to collect a present from Harrods James had ordered for Amy.

He returned the weight back to its holder and strode to the front of Sonia's machine. Matthew wrapped a sweaty towel around his shoulders after stripping off his sleeveless vest. He couldn't help but chuckle when Sonia's run began to stutter, and she pressed a button to slow her pace down.

Sonia's run slowed to a stop "Everything okay?"

"Yes, I just remembered I need to collect something for Mr North. You fancy driving me home? And you can take the Lexus home for the night; it will save you having to use the Tube. We can get something to eat, as well, if you don't have any other plans. I can fill you in a bit about the next few weeks."

"Sure, sounds good to me."

"I'll go grab a quick shower. See you out front in ten minutes."

"Give me fifteen. I will need to tame this wild hair without a hairbrush."

"I have probably got a spare in my bag; I will send it to you."

Sonia looked at him in confusion but also with a little dejection behind her eyes. "Won't your girlfriend mind me using her hairbrush?"

"No girlfriend, so that will not be a problem. Mr North likes me to be prepared, so you'll be surprised at what I keep on me."

"Really?"

"Yeah. Since Amy became a client, I have some weird stuff in there. The day after she moved in with Mr North, I gave her this questionnaire regarding details of items such as her favourite brand of lipstick, perfume, toothpaste and hairspray. She was a little shocked when she got to the question of sanitary products, but my job is to make sure she is never caught short of anything."

"That actually is being prepared. There have been numerous occasions where I have been caught short without a tampon." Sonia blushed at the direction of their conversation, Matthew liked the way even the tip of her nose went pink. "I will have to make a copy of the bag so I can be ready should she need anything as well."

"I will get one made up and put in the boot of the Lexus."

"Thank you."

"Right. Showers. If I don't get this present, my balls will be chewed off!"

Before freshening up and changing, Matthew got one of the reception ladies to take a little collection of items to Sonia.

Matthew headed to the car and climbed into the passenger's side. Now was as good a time as any to check Sonia's driving skills. She had done core competencies during the training, but Matthew wanted to see if she needed any further work. Sonia got into the driver's side after about five minutes and Matthew handed her the keys.

"Mr North's driving is awful. If I can get away with it, I am always behind the wheel." The corners of Matthew's mouth turned up into a laugh. "I won't tell you where we are going. You just have to follow my instructions."

Sonia started the engine and Matthew directed her. At one point, he asked her to overtake in a terrible situation which, if her reflexes weren't good, could have caused problems. She managed it with ease, though.

As they pulled into the Harrods car park, Matthew was pleasantly surprised at how well she had done.

"Not bad. I want to get you on a motorway soon, but your reflexes are good. Once James tells Amy about you, we can share the driving."

"Thank you." Sonia had a beaming smile on her face. Matthew hadn't really noticed before, but she was gorgeous. Sonia had pulled her brown hair down from the ponytail that she wore all day, and it framed the delicate features of her face. At twenty-six, she was seven years younger than him, but she was so fresh faced she only looked twenty. Her dark brown eyes were echoed by naturally long lashes, and he could see that she didn't wear much makeup. Sonia Anderson was a natural beauty. He turned away as she coughed softly. He had been staring at her.

"Sorry, I was distracted. As a reward, you can choose what we eat. And don't worry about the cost. Mr North is paying."

"The steakhouse here is good enough for me. I went there once before with this actress I was protecting. She was a diva, and near enough anorexic, I was surprised she met a man there. Mind you, all she ate was lettuce. Such a waste of money. What is Mr North like on that score? Does he like restaurants and eating out?"

"His mum tends to cook to for him a lot. He eats out when necessary. He is an easy boss really. The best I have ever had. He has issues like most people, but he has his head in the right place."

"He is pretty scary at first sight." They both got out of the car and walked towards the store as the valet took the car to park it. "What is it you need to collect?"

"Mr North has purchased a bag. Miss Jones doesn't really like lots of money spent on her, but he is desperate to please her. The issues with her uncle have left her a little mistrustful, but I have never seen my boss so happy than when he is with her."

"He looked comfortable but a little stressed today. I liked the fact that she didn't let him get his own way all the time."

"Yeah. He wouldn't have liked that." Matthew's face soured. "Look, Sonia, there are issues with Mr North. I can't talk to you about them without his permission but understand that everything that he does is for the best for Miss Jones. They may only be early into their relationship but he adores her. I would even go as far as to say he is in love with her."

"I understand. Don't worry. I saw the looks between them today. They are both lucky to have found each other."

"How long have you been working for Mr North? "Sonia enquired at the steakhouse, later, as she sipped her non-alcoholic Raspberry Crush and Matthew took a sip of his beer.

"About six years now. He was my first private client. We clicked, and I have just stayed. He wasn't a billionaire then, but he was up-and-coming."

"He is definitely very successful. He seems very intense, though."

"Again I can't talk about that. Your detail is to Miss Jones, not Mr North. But don't worry, his past shouldn't affect her future. Her uncle is the problem."

"Yeah, he doesn't sound like a nice man. Would Mr North ask you to make sure he didn't come near her again...?" Sonia looked up at him.

"Have you killed anyone before Sonia?"

"No, but I have seen a lot of death."

"Before this, I worked for MI5. I have been in places you can only imagine in your worst nightmares. I have killed people. To survive, I have killed more than I care to count. Mr North understands that, and leaves those decisions to me. I will only make them when I believe they are necessary. At the moment, Mr Jones is trying to save face. He lost a lot of money when Amy choose James over him. He is trying to do whatever he can to repair that reputation." The steak arrived, and they both sat back at it was served. Matthew could see that Sonia's head was full of questions. When the waiter disappeared, she leant forward.

"This isn't an ordinary security detail, is it? You have killed for him before, haven't you?"

"You know I can't confirm or deny that, Sonia. All I will say is that you need to be prepared. You need to be ready for the unexpected because no, this isn't standard protection." Matthew put a piece of steak into his mouth, and it melted away. "But I wouldn't have it any other way. Let's change the subject from me, I should be interrogating you. Tell me about yourself?"

Matthew knew about Sonia anyway; --she'd had a full security check with MI5 before he even considered employing her. Some of the stuff had been hard reading, especially the part where her father had killed her mother.

"Not much to tell really. I grew up on a farm in the Lake District. My mother died when I was young so my aunt took over my care."

"I am sorry to hear of your mother's death. That must have been hard. How old were you?"

"I was seven."

"Very young." Matthew kept his face neutral but welcoming, to invite her to open up to him.

"You don't need to do the interrogation techniques on me you know. I make no secret of the fact my father killed my mother. He is in prison for life without parole as a result. I don't see him. I don't want to see him. I have no father as far as I am concerned. But I suspect you probably know all this, and more, about me." She brought the steak up to her mouth again and swallowed it down.

"I am sorry, that was rude of me. Yes, my spy training took over. It is all I have known since I left school. Sometimes I let it rule me a little. You must tell me to shut up if it happens again. This working with a partner is new to me as well. I spent a lot of time alone when I was on duty." Matthew cursed himself as he spoke. He was opening himself up to interrogation. He didn't do this. This is the reason he kept away from women. They made him talk. Yeah when James had gone to clubs in the past he had joined him and enjoyed the company of the ladies there. He and James worked well as a duo of Masters but Matthew was glad that James had found Amy now and that his boss had become effectively celibate since Lanzarote. It meant Matthew could just focus on the protection side of things. But this woman here, in front of him, was destroying that. He knew Sonia had seen the way into changing the conversation around to him, despite all her first day nerves she was as excellent in her techniques as he was. That is why he had chosen her. Matthew pulled his phone from his pocket, and pretended he had received a message.

"I am really sorry. James wants the bag now. I am going to have to go." He pulled out his wallet and threw a hundred pounds on the table. "Order yourself dessert as well and then take the Audi home. I will get a cab. See you tomorrow." Without letting her reply, he stood and took a coward's retreat as fast as possible. He couldn't trust another woman. Last time it had almost got him killed. He wouldn't make that mistake again.

CHAPTER THREE

Sonia

Sonia jumped into the passenger seat of the Bentley. Matthew was driving, and they exchanged weary glances. Sonia had just broken cover and revealed herself to Amy. The poor woman was being hounded by the press for comment on her relationship with Mr North. She was on the edge of the Diana Memorial Fountain and being pushed further back; in danger of falling. Sonia had had no choice. Matthew had been with the car.

As the car pulled under the house in Knightsbridge, Miss Jones got out and stomped off without a word.

"Is he going to be mad at me?" Sonia got out of the car and looked at Matthew. She had been working with Mr North for a month now and had seen his temper on more than one occasion. Amy seemed to be the only one who could melt it; however, given the mood, she was in, Sonia doubted that would happen anytime soon.

"You did what was necessary to protect Miss Jones. Mr North will understand that. It was his choice not to tell Amy about you, and he needs to deal with the consequences of that decision." Matthew locked the car and headed for the stairs. "Come on, you might as well come with me. I have my own rooms; I will make you a drink while we wait for the fireworks."

Sonia hadn't spoken to Matthew about anything other than business since she told him about her parents. She couldn't blame him--he wasn't the first, and he wouldn't be the last. The thought, however, of trying to make pleasant conversation with him while worrying if she had a job filled her with dread.

"It is okay; I should go and get my car. I will do that

while we are waiting."

The warmth of his fingers wrapped around hers and he pulled her to him. Shivers of electricity flooded her body.

"Stay."

Sonia pulled her hand away, she was still angry with him.

"It is okay; you don't have to be polite just because things are messed up. We can stick to business mode." She pulled the strap of her handbag over her head, and made for the exit to the garage. Before she knew it, though, Matthew was in front of her, his broad arms folded across his chest, and a stern expression on his face.

"Upstairs, now!"

"No!"

"Sonia, I will not ask you again!"

"Look I get it. My father killed my mother. It makes you uncomfortable around me. It is nothing new. Just let me go."

Matthew didn't move. He studied her, and she felt so small. Slowly, he stepped aside, but as she went to pass him, he grabbed her, tossed her over his shoulder like a rag doll, and pinned her so she couldn't move. She was better trained than that. How had she allowed him to get her into this position? Matthew went up the stairs, and his big boots clomped on the marble floor.

"Matthew put me down!" She tried to thump his back. If she could reach her gun, she would shoot the bastard in the foot. "Matthew!"

"No!"

"Damn it. You may be my boss but you can't manhandle me!"

"Who says!"

"Err... government rules on sexual harassment in the workplace."

"I told you, Sonia, this is no standard job. The rules don't apply here."

What the hell did he mean by that?

Matthew dropped her to the floor without any grace or ceremony, when they stopped outside a doorway in a long corridor. From nearby, she could hear James and Amy shouting at each other. Sonia got up and tried to escape again, but Matthew just pinned her against the door with his muscular body. Damn. All her fantasising over his taut abs and six-, no make that eight-, pack.

"Stay still. You don't move!" Matthew turned his attention back to the door. Sonia just stood still. Jesus. God complex or what. She bet his dick was tiny, and he was making up for it with the attitude. When the door was open, he stood back, releasing her and motioned for her to go in.

"Why?" She clenched her teeth and glared at him.

"Because I want to talk to you."

"I want you to learn some manners, but I am not sure that's going to happen. I can see why you and Mr North get on." Matthew growled. God, the man was an animal. Suddenly losing her job didn't really seem to bother her. She wasn't sure she wanted it anymore. She went into the room. Before Matthew knew what was happening, Sonia swung around, kicked her leg out, and sent him flying onto the floor. She pulled the gun out of its holster and pointed it at his head.

"Now, I still have the safety on, but unless you tell me what is going on, I will take it off. And I don't care what you say about that breaking your stupid rules or being irresponsible. I happen to think you swinging me over your shoulder and demanding I go into your bedroom is pretty fucking stupid as well!"

"This isn't my bedroom!" Matthew didn't flinch, although he did look a little surprised to be flat on his back on the floor. "When I asked you here it was to explain." Matthew started to get up from the floor. Sonia let him, but didn't holster the weapon. "I don't find it uncomfortable that your father killed your mother. In fact, if you ever want to talk about it, then I am here for you. I have issues, Sonia, they stem from my Secret Service work. I am so sorry if you felt that my silence was your fault. Please, put the gun away. Let's go sit down and talk. This is obviously a big issue for you. The fact you've drawn a weapon on me for saying it, does worry me. It would seem a little bit of an overreaction."

"I drew the gun because you're a prat who picked me up and carried me over your shoulder!"

Matthew got to his feet and started laughing.

"I am sorry Sonia." He took a step back and held his hands up. "I know the details of your parents' case and a lot of what happened to you afterwards. I made it my business to know when James agreed to your employment. It is the only way I can protect him."

"You know everything?"

"I don't know your feelings, but I know the facts."

Sonia retracted the gun and placed it on a table beside her.

"He was an alcoholic."

"Your father?"

"Yes."

Sonia sat down. She had never spoken to anyone about any of this. Matthew sat beside her on the sofa. He didn't touch her, but she could sense his presence.

"Did your parents argue a lot?"

"Always. Every night he would come home drunk and complain about something. He didn't have the right dinner, or it wasn't warm enough. She hadn't washed his favourite clothes for the morning. I was being too noisy and needed to be quieted. He would spend all his days on the farm and would get off around seven and would disappear to the local pub. He never drove—just walked across the fields. One night, I remember him being brought home by a couple of the farmhands. He had fallen in the snow and slid down an embankment. He had bruising and blood all over his face. He was swearing and shouting at my mother. Do you know what she was doing?"

"I don't."

"She was trying to clean him up. I remember him smacking her across the face, stumbling into the bedroom, and locking the door. She spent the night in my room with me, we woke up to blood from her lip on my pillow." Sonia looked up at Matthew. She never even talked to her counsellors like this. Damn him." I really need to go and get the car." Sonia stood up and walked away from him towards the door.

"Sonia, what happened the night your mother died?"

She turned to face him. "I am not ready to face that."

Matthew came closer, She could smell his spicy cologne.

"Okay, I will not ask any more questions. Sonia, there is something you should know. The file I got about you said you could be a liability because you don't talk about your feelings. You kept them bottled up inside you like a ticking time bomb. I know that only too well, it is one of the reasons that I chose you for this job. James, Mr North, he is a man with many issues, and I am the same. I don't know Amy that well yet, but I see the same with her. Together, I would like to believe that we can heal each other."

"That is a rather optimistic view of life." Sonia leant in, breathing in his scent again.

"I need to have some hopes of humanity, or I may as well take my gun and go for a rather long walk."

"Please don't do that."

"Why?"

"I think Mr North needs you. You're a good 'south' to his 'north'"

"Please, I have heard enough of the psycho drivel to last me a lifetime." Matthew wrapped his arms around her waist and pulled her toward him. "Use me, Sonia, I want to help you get over this. I may have only known you a month, but you're a wonderful bodyguard, and you could do some great things with your life. Don't let the past hold you back."

"Says the man that has barely spoken to me the last month because I am a woman and turned the conversation around to him and not me."

"No, because I am a man and as such I am a stupid fool. Ignore that!" Matthew leant further over her so that their lips were only inches apart. What the hell was happening here? She could feel her lady parts beginning to flutter with excitement. Hello, get a grip, this is your boss. He is just trying to find out what he wants about you to manipulate you. That is what men do. "Sonia, one final question for tonight. Will you answer it?

"That would depend on what it is."

"It is about your parents."

"Then I can't guarantee that I will answer it. But you can try."

"Did you see your father murder your mother?"

The world went quiet. The dreaded question. Everyone always asked her that, her aunt, the police, the counsellors, even the children at her school. She pulled away from Matthew. She wouldn't let him be the same.

"It's the one thing missing from your records. The one question that you've always been asked, but you never answer."

"Matthew, please."

"Sonia, answer me."

A knock came at the door of Matthew's apartment. Sonia breathed a sigh of relief. What happened that night was hidden behind closed doors.

"Matthew, is Sonia with you?" James' voice came from the other side of the door.

"Yes, boss." Matthew gave her a look that said this isn't over before striding to the door and opening it. Both James and Amy stood the other side. They stepped into the room and James pushed Amy forward.

"Say it," James spoke with stern authority. Amy looked ashamed.

"Hello Sonia. I want to apologise for my behaviour earlier. If James had told me about you, then I would have been a little bit friendlier when you interceded with that nasty reporter. I hope that you can forgive my rudeness. I am sorry."

"That is okay Miss Jones, I am sorry to have given you such a shock as well. I hope that in future we are able to work together with fewer problems. "Sonia stepped forward, still shaking from her encounter with Matthew. She needed to sort herself out. No weakness--she couldn't afford to show that, it would only lead to pain.

CHAPTER FOUR

Matthew

The flight to India reached cruising altitude, and the seatbelts sign flashed off. Matthew undid his belt and got up. He leant over to Sonia who already had her headphones on, lying back on the seat with her eyes shut, her half-drunk glass of champagne was in her hand. He touched her gently, and her eyes sprang open. She lifted the ear of one of her headphones off. "Is everything ok?"

"I just need to go and speak to the stewardess. Do you want anything?"

"No, I am going to stick to a movie until dinner. Or do I need to check on Miss Jones?"

"You're fine. Rest. We will have a full day when we arrive in India. Mr North booked out the whole of first class so they could be alone."

"Oh. I better leave them to it then." Sonia blushed.

Matthew nodded to Sonia and headed off to the find the stewardess who was looking after the first class. After finding her, and parting with a considerable sum of money, Matthew was safe in his knowledge that his boss could get up to whatever he wanted to and wouldn't be disturbed. And it wouldn't be reported in the newspapers tomorrow. He returned to his seat and Sonia pulled her headphones off.

"Did you find the stewardess?"

"Yes, everything is sorted. We should have a peaceful flight. What are you watching?"

"The latest Renegade film. I saw it at the cinema when it came out."

"Good choice. What do you think of the lead actor?"

"Grayson Moore? He is good. Needs a bit more realism

in some of his stunts. They sometimes feel too staged. A side effect of the job, I guess."

Matthew let out a barking laugh. "I thought you might have known. I was testing you. James' sister, Sophie, is engaged to Mr Moore. They are marrying at Christmas."

Sonia's mouth fell. Matthew couldn't help but laugh again. "Seriously? Please, you mustn't tell him I think his stunts aren't that good."

"Oh no, that's too priceless not to tell him. He'll tease you rotten!"

Sonia went bright and she looked cute when she was embarrassed. He guessed that was why he had taken to teasing her whenever he had the opportunity.

"It is okay; I have told him the same thing before anyway. He blamed the stunt coordinator. Apparently, he needs everything to look a specific way for the film. If Grayson had his way, he would just go for it and figure out the fight with the other guy on his own."

"Now that would make the films a lot better. Maybe you and I should take over as his stunt coordinator!"

"What, and miss listening to Amy and James having sex in an aeroplane bathroom." Matthew laughed but right on cue came a carnal giggle from Amy and a slam against the wall from within the toilet.

"Has he done this before?"

"What?"

"The mile-high club?"

"No, that's a first for him actually. I like to be one step ahead of him, second-guess what he'll want."

"You're good. How did you learn everything?"

"I see what you're doing."

"What?"

"Turning the conversation around to me."

"I wasn't."

"Don't lie. Your nose crinkles when you do." Matthew pulled his foot stool down and saw Sonia watching him as the stewardess brought him another glass of wine. "So are you going to tell me?"

"Tell you what?"

"Did you see your father kill your mother?" Matthew kept his voice calm.

"Matthew, please, I don't want to talk about this. Not here at least."

"Now is a good as time as any. We have ten hours stuck on this plane together. I don't watch films, so you're going to talk to me."

"Has anyone ever told you that you're really bossy?"

"I get told most days, but I know you like it, really, just from the way you obey me." Sonia blushed again, and Matthew felt a strange stirring. "Come on, answer me."

Sonia looked away and out of the window for a few moments, and Matthew didn't speak. When she turned back, she had tears in her eyes.

"Yes. Yes, I did." Her words were quiet, and she faltered but continued. "It was his birthday. My dad had been down at the pub most of the day. Mum made a special meal for us so we could celebrate it together, however it was late when he got home. He asked why I was still up, and mum explained. I just stood there cowering. My dad actually smiled and told mum that was very thoughtful. He took a seat at the table, and I tentatively brought him a book over to read. He read it to me, one of the things he always did, drunk or not. His voice was slurred, and he stank of beer, but I loved the closeness with him. Mum brought the food over to the table. Pie and chips. His favourite." She turned away again. After a few minutes, she turned back again, took a sip of her champagne, before pushing it away as if it were poison. "Everything was perfect. Until my dad cut into his pie. It was chicken instead of beef. He began to shout at my mum, calling her names which, as a seven-year-old I shouldn't have known, but were already second nature to me. Mum started to cry. I got down from my chair and went to her. I looked up at my dad and said he wasn't very nice, mummy was only trying to make his birthday special for him, and she had spent all afternoon making the pie. I will always remember the look on his face."

"Sonia, you're doing so well. I know this is hard, but I am here to listen."

She nodded, "He flew at me and smacked me in the face. He was about to kick me, but my mum jumped at him and began to hit him on the back. He turned and punched her in the stomach. He was shouting at the top his voice, calling us both names, I scrambled into a corner of the kitchen. My mother, she should have just laid there and taken the beating, but she didn't. She fought back and told him she was leaving him. She would never let him hit her daughter." Tears were tumbling down Sonia's face now. Matthew sat at her feet, holding her hand. "Dad picked one of the sharp knives up off the table. When he finished, blood covered his shirt. He looked at me, turned, and ran. I haven't seen him since. He was sentenced to twenty-five years in prison. I know he'll be eligible for parole soon, but I don't think I can ever face that." Sonia slid off her chair and into Matthew's arms. He enveloped her while she cried.

CHAPTER FIVE

Sonia

Sonia shifted on the sun lounger so that she was more in the shade. Amy was swimming lengths of the infinity pool at the top of the hotel while James was with the hotel's manager, completing business before they flew to the Maldives tomorrow. Sonia wore a lightweight trouser suit. It wasn't designer, but it was tasteful. Amy had told her she didn't need to wear suits at all, but it was all she had ever known as a bodyguard. Maybe they could go shopping when they got back to London and find something Amy felt was more suitable.

Sonia was planning for this job to be long term. She never did that. All her previous posts were short and sweet.

The door opened to the roof top pool, and Sonia's hand instinctively went for her Glock. She relaxed when she saw it was Matthew. She smiled across at him, and he winked back and took a protective stance which meant he had been dismissed by Mr North and would take on responsibility for Miss Jones.

Amy noticed him as well and pulled up to the side. She placed her arms on the edge of the infinity pool and started to tread water.

"Do you think I can get James to build one of these on the roof of the house in Knightsbridge?"

Sonia took off her sensible shoes and jacket; rolled up the end of her trousers and dipped her toes in the water.

"Would he be getting some of the lovely weather back to England as well?"

"Unfortunately, he keeps telling me he isn't God, even though he acts like it, and he can't control that sort of thing. Yet."

"I don't know what you see in him, Amy. He can't control the weather. He is useless."

"He is just so incredible in bed. I guess I will have to settle with that for now."

"I am not sure I need to know that about my employer!"

"Oh come on. I think you've heard us the last few nights!"

"Ear plugs. It is the first thing you get given at Bodyguard school!"

"Bodyguard school? You mean there is such a place?" Amy looked at her with mocking shock.

"No, but James employs Matthew for a reason. I was thoroughly put through my paces to get this job. I think his requirements are stricter than those for the Queen herself!"

Amy looked over to where Matthew stood, and he did a little theatrical bow. She then quietened her voice as she spoke to Sonia.

"So, Matthew?"

"Yes, Miss Jones? Mr Carter, he is your and James' bodyguard and my boss."

"I have noticed the way he looks at you..."

Sonia prayed that Matthew couldn't hear what they were saying. He was sexy, but she wasn't going to admit that about her boss. All he was doing was looking after her and making sure she was able to do her job properly. He had already made it clear to her that he kept himself to himself. "Matthew is probably looking at me because I don't do everything the way he likes."

'No, I think he wants you to do lots of things the way he likes them and not just as a bodyguard!"

"Amy!"

"Hey, I am in love, and I know the signs."

"It is just a working relationship. He helped me overcome something that was holding me back. That is all. Besides, we wouldn't have time to protect you and James from mishaps if we were making lovey-dovey eyes at each other all the time."

"True. And James can really get himself into trouble. Okay. I will leave it for now!" Amy pushed off the side and swam to the steps to get out of the pool. Sonia picked up her dressing gown, ready to hand to her but before she could, the door to the pool area opened again, and James' voice bellowed out.

"Amy. What the fuck are you wearing?"

Sonia looked towards Matthew and could see him sigh.

"It is called a bikini James." Amy reached out to take her dressing gown. With her back to James, Amy rolled her eyes. Sonia tried not to laugh.

"It is a strip of fabric that shows off your body. Your body is for my eyes only!"

"And that's why the pool was only available to me while I was swimming. Sonia and Matthew ensured it."

James looked towards Matthew.

"Why didn't you tell me that she was swimming half naked?"

"Sorry boss, I did as she asked--cleared the pool and had Sonia stand guard so nobody could see her."

"What you should have done was buy her a swimming costume that covered her from head to foot. They have them here."

"Yes, boss."

"James, I am not wearing a burkini!"

James turned back to Amy. "Get in the bedroom now!"

"James!"

"NOW!" His angry voice echoed against the wind protected area.

"Fine. Matthew, Sonia. Thank you for carrying out my request even if Mr 'I have a stick up my arse' doesn't agree with them."

"Amy!" James glared at his girlfriend, but Sonia couldn't help but notice the tenting in his trousers that indicated how Amy was to be punished for flashing her flesh.

"You're such an annoying old man sometimes!" Amy walked through the door allowing it to bang behind her.

"Matthew, I have finished all the work I need to do here. I am going to spend the next twenty-four hours with my girlfriend reminding her of my rules and how she is punished if she disobeys them. We will not leave the bedroom. Arrange for guards to be placed outside. You and Sonia can have time off for your own leisure.

"I will arrange things at once, James."

"Have fun." James looked over to Sonia and smiled. Sonia controlled her urge to roll her eyes.

James disappeared through the door, and Matthew took a few steps closer to her.

"Is it me or are they trying to match make?"

"I thought you might be worried about them arguing and what James would do to Amy."

"Arguing is foreplay for them. I am not stupid. It is nothing like what my parents used to do. Anyway. Back to my question."

"Yes, they are matchmaking. But this doesn't have to be anything more than you want it to be. Look, I will be honest. I am not a relationship type of guy. I am married to my job, and I always will be. If you want to have fun while we have some free time together, then I am more than happy to do so. But love and all that stuff? It isn't going to happen."

"Ok" Sonia wasn't ready for a relationship either. She still had things hidden from him. "So, this friendship, fun thing. What are you thinking about?"

"You ever been on a motorbike?"

"A few times, why?"

"It is one of the fastest ways to travel in India. Do you fancy going cross-country for the day? There are a couple of things you need to experience before we leave."

"Sounds fun. What do I need to do?"

"Go back to your room. I will organise some leathers and get them sent up."

They walked into the air-conditioned hallway, a welcome relief from the already hot day outside, and Matthew pressed the call button on the lift. The elevator arrived, and they stepped in. Sonia only had one floor to go, but the rooftop could only be accessed by special cards inserted into the lift control pad. Apparently, this was a security precaution and meant that room keys only allowed access to a particular floor. It was normal and put in place in hotels of this quality after the Mumbai terrorist attacks.

"It is a place called Pondicherry. It is where the French settled when they came here."

The lift dinged for Sonia's floor, and she spoke as she got out.

"How long does it take?"

"Five hours the way I drive."

"Five hours!" She spat out her answer!

The lift doors started to shut.

"Pack an overnight bag."

"Wait. What!"

The doors closed.

Sonia drifted back to the suite she occupied with everyone else. She could already hear Amy being punished by James. Sonia opened the door to her room and sat down on her bed. She was in a bit of a daze. All she could hear was Matthew saying pack an overnight bag, his gravelly voice promising something. They were going somewhere alone together. He had said he didn't want a relationship, just fun. Did he mean sexual fun? Maybe with all the teasing he thought that's what she wanted.

Oh God. Could she change her mind and say she didn't feel like going now?

Sonia laid her gun on the dressing table, undid the buttons of her shirt and let it fall to the floor. She then kicked off her shoes and lowered her trousers and folded them back into the suitcase. Her room had an ornately carved full-length mirror in it. She hated mirrors, she had a small solitary one in her flat back in England that she used to put makeup on and do her hair but other than that she avoided them wherever she could. She forced herself to open her eyes as she stood in front of this, though. She was being foolhardy. Matthew would never want her. Nobody would ever want her in that way. She was damaged. The ugly red scars that marked the top of her thighs and her buttocks were all that she could see when she looked at the full reflection of her naked body. This is why she avoided physical intimacy. Nobody wanted someone as grotesque as she was. It was the lasting legacy of her father and the way he killed her mother.

A gentle knock came to the door, and she pulled a gown on. As she opened the door, Matthew stood there with biker's leathers.

"That was quick." She forced the happy tone into her voice. She could tell that Matthew was not fooled, though. He instantly frowned.

"Is this too much?"

"Pardon?"

"Going away for the night? You must still be tired after the plane journey. Maybe we could just go for a little ride and then have dinner in the city. The Bangalore Palace can be beautiful." That would be the safer option and definitely the most sensible the way she was feeling, but something snapped within her at that moment

"No, this might be the only chance I get to see India so I want to see as much of it as I can. I will be ready in half an hour."

"Okay." He put the leathers down just inside her door and then rested his hands on her shoulders. A sudden heat surged through her body. "I promise you, nothing will happen that we both don't agree on together. I won't hurt a woman again."

Sonia tilted her head. "Again?"

"Again?"

"You said you won't hurt a woman again."

"Sorry." He pointed toward Amy and James' room where the bed was now ramming against the wall and Amy was screaming. "I can't think straight with that going on. Half an hour, and we will get out of here and can explore. You happy with that?"

"Yes."

"Good." Matthew let go of her and walked off to his room.

Again? Why had he said again?

CHAPTER SIX

Matthew

Matthew felt Sonia's slight arms tighten around his waist as he pulled the brand new Triumph Street Twin to a halt. One good thing about working for Mr James North: if you wanted something, then it was given to you. In a matter of minutes. Matthew stopped at a Hindu temple.

They both removed their helmets and placed them on the bike.

"We won't stop here long, but I wanted to show you something."

"We can stay as long as you want. It is a fantastic place. Nothing like the English churches. It is all so colourful."

Matthew looked up at the unusual statue of the deity Ganesha that dominated the entrance of the temple. It was indeed very different to the bland churches in the UK. The four-armed and elephant-headed god was painted in vibrant pink with gold accents. On either side were two worshipers who had gold all over them. The temple itself was decorated in blues, purples, greens and yellow. It was a spectacular sight.

"Come," Matthew reached out and took Sonia's hand, "I want to show you inside, but we need to take our boots off and leave them outside. It is polite." Matthew pointed towards a pile of sandals that were scattered on the floor.

"How do they actually remember where they put their shoes?"

"I have no idea, but they do. Chaos works in India!"

"It certainly does."

They removed their boots and left them by the bike rather than on the mound of flip-flops.

"Ganesha is the god of wisdom and intellect, isn't he?"

"Yes." Matthew looked at Sonia as she questioned him.

"Are you hoping that maybe this visit gives me more wisdom to follow your high intellect and rules?"

"I think you might need to stay here for a month for that to happen."

Sonia whacked out a hand into his hard bicep.

"Hey!" They walked into the temple together, and the hum of people worshiping filled their ears. Matthew looked over to Sonia and saw a look of wonder on her face. She often looked so lost, but when she smiled she was the most beautiful woman on the planet.

"Do you think they will mind if I take a few photographs?" She pulled out her phone.

"Of course not. I will make a substantial donation when we leave, so we can do anything we want here within reason." Money still talked in India.

"I left my rupees in my bag on the bike."

"It is fine. You can pay me back later."

"Thank you." Sonia smiled again and turned to take her photos.

Matthew stepped back against the wall and tried desperately to focus on something other than her tight backside in her skin-tight leather trousers as she wiggled away.

"Oh my God. There is an elephant in here." Everyone stopped what they were doing and stared at Sonia, who instantly turned a bright shade of red. Matthew just shook his head before pushing off the wall.

"Sorry, the first time she has seen an elephant." The staring crowd murmured and returned to their worshipping. "You want to go and see the elephant. It is actually the reason I brought you here." He held his hand out to her, but she didn't take it. Instead, she buried her head in his broad chest. Matthew felt his breath catch.

"I feel so stupid."

"It is okay." Matthew stroked her hair. "They are probably used to it. They don't advertise the fact there is an elephant in the Temple!"

Sonia, lifted her head, and he met her questioning eyes. He wanted to lean in and kiss her; her lips were so inviting, so tempting.

"Sorry." Sonia pulled away from him and nervously fiddled with a strand of her hair. "Yes, let's go see the elephant. What is so special about it?"

Matthew coughed as he stepped back to try and draw air back into his lungs. He reached into his pocket and pulled out some rupees.

"Go up to him and wait. Hold this flat in the palm of your hand."

"Seriously?"

"Seriously."

"Okay, but if I get trampled I will come back to haunt you."

"Go!" Matthew laughed, the unease of moments earlier lost as they both strode over to the elephant and Sonia stood in front of it as she was told to. Matthew watched as the elephant brought its enormous trunk up and swiped it over Sonia's face. The elephant then took the money, gave it to its handler, and turned its head to the next patron. Sonia turned back to him, a baffled expression on her face.

"Ok, what was that?"

"You were just blessed by an elephant."

"Blessed? I thought he was giving me a wash."

"He is only slobbery with the ones he likes."

"That is good to know." She laughed and wiped her face on the cuff of her jacket. "Do they do this in many temples?"

"Sometimes elephants, sometimes cows. Animals are sacred and worshipped here."

"I actually think I enjoyed that more than my holy communion."

Matthew just shook his head again before calling over one of the priests.

"Hi, I have a new bike outside. Can we get a puja for it please?"

He pulled out his wallet and handed a wad of rupees to

the priest.

"Of course, Sir. I will arrange it at once." The man scurried off.

"Um. What is a puja?"

"A way of making sure we get back to Bangalore in time for the plane tomorrow. James can be rather stressed if I make him late. Follow me."

Sonia followed as Matthew grabbed her hand again and he led her back outside the temple. A man was placing a flowered garland over the front of the bike. He then threw a handful of petals over the rest of it. Matthew pressed his hands together and presented a courtesy Namaste greeting to the priest. Matthew felt Sonia tense beside him as the priest picked up a coconut shell and set it alight. He then chanted as he waved it over the bike. He blew the flame out and smashed the coconut on the ground.

"This is the fun part." Matthew handed Sonia her helmet and boots and put his back on. "Back on the bike." Matthew manoeuvred the bike to ride off but waited until the priest had placed limes under the wheels. "Hold on!" He switched the engine on, and the bike sped away, crushing the limes. He could hear Sonia chuckling behind him.

"That was mad!" She spoke into the microphone in her helmet, and it echoed in his.

"It is bonkers but very important. Did you enjoy that place?"

"I loved it. I can't wait to see more of Pondicherry."

Matthew turned the bike on what would probably be a B road in England into the French District of the city. He pulled up outside a whitewashed villa neatly erected on a set grid place. The French Quarter was formally laid out.

Matthew stretched and flexed his neck as he got off the bike. It had been a long ride, and he needed a warm shower. He grabbed his bag and handed Sonia's to her.

"I feel like I am in France, not India."

"It really does feel like that doesn't it?" Matthew guided her towards the entrance to the hotel.

"Ma'am, you must go this way, please."

They both looked up to the attendant dressed in traditional dress.

"Of course, you have to go with the woman. It is only for the start, they need to do a quick security check, and then we can meet when we get in there." Matthew had forgotten about the segregation in some places in India.

"Why can't we go together?"

"Women are respected for virtue in this country. Their dignity is maintained when they have to be searched. It isn't done everywhere, but this hotel apparently chooses to do so." He pointed towards a little curtain. "I will wait for you just the other side. Please, don't worry."

"Okay."

Matthew breezed through his security check, he had left his gun back in Bangalore. He felt naked without it, but he didn't need it here. His hands were more than a capable weapon. And the knife that he had hidden in his boot wasn't picked up. He strode to the desk and gave them his name. He might as well get the keys to their rooms, Sonia might be a while, stuck behind a woman with three children in the queue. He always felt it a little unfair that the children frequently ended up with the woman while she was trying to get herself checked and them, surely her husband could have taken one of them.

"Welcome, Mr. Carter. Can I get your credit card, please? I have put you in your usual room."

"Merci Sabine. Where is Miss Anderson's room?"

"Miss Anderson's room?" Sabine looked confused. "I had the message that you wanted one room. I am so sorry. We are fully booked."

Sonia appeared behind him.

"I can phone around a few hotels for you Mr Carter but there is a big festival on tonight, and the city is very busy."

"Does the room have a sofa or twin beds?" Sonia asked

"It has a sofa."

"I will take the couch."

"You'll not!" His protective side came out. "I will take it."

"You won't fit."

"I could see if we could get an extra bed put in the room, Mr Carter?" Sabine interjected.

"See to it at once, please." Matthew picked up the key card and stomped to the elevator.

"Matthew, I don't snore, you know. And I will even wear PJ's, so I don't give you a fright."

"I am sorry. I didn't plan this."

"I know. It is just an error; we didn't exactly know we were coming here till a few hours ago."

"Thanks for offering to share. If they can't find a bed, then I will take the couch." Matthew was going to be adamant on this. He was responsible for her safety while she was here and he wouldn't allow her to sleep on a couch.

"If they can't find a bed, we can share the double together. Come on, let's get changed, and then I want to find some French food. I have had enough of curries for this trip!" Sonia swiped the key from his hand and ran ahead to the bedroom. Matthew let out a long exhalation of air. It was going to be a long night. A very long and very tortuous night.

CHAPTER SEVEN

Sonia

Sonia stepped out of the walk-in shower and wrapped the fluffy white towel around her body. After five hours on the back of a motorbike, in often very dusty and hot conditions, she really needed to have a wash. She hadn't minded the journey though as she had seen so much of India. This area was famous for its old ambassador cars and she had definitely seen a lot of them. The poverty in the country had struck her, though. It was everywhere, there was an immense divide between the rich and the poor. She wondered if it would ever really change.

Her ears pricked up as she heard Matthew on the phone. Matthew hadn't been joking, he really was married to the job. He was obviously talking to James on the phone from the nature of the conversation. Even when he was given a day to himself, he was still checking on his boss and making sure everything was safe and in place for him.

Sonia took the purple A-line dress from the coat hanger on the back of the door and put it on. She really didn't know why she had let Amy talk her into bringing it. She shoved her feet into a pair of high heels. She put a little bit of blusher on her cheeks and some mascara over her eyelashes. A quick towel dry of her hair and a comb through, and she was ready. Tentatively, she opened the door, Matthew turned his head to her and stopped speaking.

"James, I have to go." Matthew hung up. "You look beautiful."

"Amy made me borrow it. I should have just brought some trousers and a top. I feel silly."

"Why?" Matthew was dressed in a pair of tailored black casual trousers and had a short sleeved shirt on. As he stepped closer, Sonia could smell his spicy aftershave filling her nostrils. She loved that smell, it was quintessentially Matthew.

"I don't really wear dresses."

"You should. Honestly, you look beautiful." Matthew was directly in front of her now. Sonia bit lightly on her lip as she felt Matthew's eyes travel all over her body.

"I will just get my bag, and I will be ready to go."

"Yeah." Matthew almost ran back over to his side of the room and grabbed the room key and his wallet. "The restaurant is a couple of minutes' walk. It is called the Hotel Du L'Orient and is set in a little courtyard. Very typically French.

"I am looking forward to it, however, if the menu isn't in English then you're telling me what is on it!"

"No worries. Je vais vous assurer que vous mangez les escargots." Matthew smirked at her.

"Ok, what did you say?"

"I will make sure you eat the snails."

"I think I will ask the waiter to translate instead!"

"Fine, if you want les cuisses de grenouilles."

"Oh God. What is that?"

"Frog's legs!"

"Ok, I think I might ask for a curry."

"Honestly the food is good. They have fantastic steaks."

Sonia's stomach rumbled at the thought of a steak; its juices oozing from within a pepper sauce.

"Let's go. I am starving!" She grabbed her handbag and stamped her foot impatiently as Matthew messed around with his shirt.

"Patience. It is still early!"

"Unless you want me to start gnawing your arm off then I suggest you hurry up!"

"Women!" Sonia watched as Matthew tucked his wallet and his phone into the back pockets of his trousers. "Come on, then!"

Matthew was indeed right about the restaurant. It had

food that melted in Sonia's mouth and tantalised all her senses. For her dessert, she had had a Pineapple Ravioli with a salted caramel crumb. She had felt like she was floating away in a warm hug of deliciousness. Matthew had laughed as she had moaned her satisfaction and questioned whether she was acting out the scene from When Harry Met Sally.

As well as the mouth-watering food, the company was pleasant, and Sonia was extremely surprised to find the normally closed-book Matthew opening up. He was still very cagey, but she had managed to learn that he had grown up in Hampshire to a father who was a lawyer and a French mother, who was a teacher in the local secondary school. He had one brother, Christopher who was a lawyer like his father. She had the feeling Matthew was a bit of a black sheep in the family. She asked him about his time in MI5, but he had become more reserved, so she had changed it to their hobbies. Both of them were big Star Wars geeks, and when Sonia found out James had taken Matthew to watch the last one being filmed and even got him a small part in it, she was extremely jealous. The closest she had ever gotten to anything like that was a Star Wars convention in London where she had dressed up as Princess Leia and had a photograph taken with an Ewok.

As they returned to the room for the evening, another bed still hadn't been set up.

"I will get on to the reception." Matthew picked up the phone with an angry frown on his face.

"Matthew, honestly don't worry. We need to be up early in the morning to get back to Bangalore in time for the flight. It has already gone ten; if you call them, it will take another hour at least. The bed is more than big enough for two. We can put a pillow in the middle. I trust you with my virtue!"

He put the phone down. "You trust me, but I'm not sure if I trust you. I mean, look how sexy my body is." Matthew turned and wiggled his backside at her. Matthew was always so imposing and stern when on duty, but this relaxed version was really tempting.

"Oh God. I don't know if I can sleep in the same bed as that gorgeous arse and not want to bite it." She pretended to roll her eyes.

"You can eat all you want, babe!" Sonia gulped as she saw Matthew's eyes darken. She wasn't sure if Matthew sensed her nervousness, but he bowed his head and handed her the pyjamas she had left on the bed earlier. "I have some calls I need to make to check everything is ready for Mr North in the Maldives. You head to sleep; they have a work area; I can make the calls there so I don't disturb you."

"Okay." She turned towards the bathroom. The door silently clicked behind her.

In silence, Sonia got ready for bed, trying to understand what had just happened. Did she want Matthew? Had he really sensed she was worried about being alone with him? Or was she just not his type? Sonia was the daughter of a murderer. She had lank brown hair which just hung there, and she could do nothing with it. Her bottom and hips were too big, and her breasts were almost non-existent. She wasn't beautiful as Amy was. She was plain, and then there were her scars.

Yes, just one look in the mirror told her that she was someone Matthew could never be interested in. She climbed into bed and cried. She must have fallen asleep because the next thing she knew was Matthew tapping her lightly on the shoulder.

"Sonia, I am sorry to wake you, but I want to show you something. This is one of the main reasons I come to Pondicherry."

She turned over and rubbed her eyes, still sore from crying. "What time is it? It is still dark."

"It is just before six. We have to leave at eight to make sure we get back. Are you okay to get up?"

"Yes, it is fine, I'm just a bit achy after the bike ride yesterday. Been a while since I have done that. What is it you wanted to show me?"

"Come to the window." Matthew got out of the bed, and all he was wearing was a pair of tight boxer shorts. Every other inch of his muscular body was on display. Sonia felt that view right between her legs. He did indeed have a backside she wanted to sink her teeth into. "Come on, you don't want to miss it!"

She pulled the blankets back, swung her legs out of the bed, and strode to the window. The hotel was on the seafront, and the sun was coming up, its pink, purple and amber tones appearing over the horizon. It was vast and unimpeded by clouds like it would be in England. It felt like she could almost reach out and touch it. In fact, she brought her hand up against the window pane. Matthew moved in behind her, and she felt his warm breath on the back of her head. His hand slid over the curve of her hip. His pressed his body into her, and she could feel his cock starting to twitch awake against her back. She turned in his arms and looked up at him. Neither of them spoke.

Matthew brought his lips down on hers. Sparks of electricity surged through her body as she parted them slightly. Matthew lifted her off her feet, and she wrapped her legs around his waist. Jesus. His cock was rock solid underneath her. He laid her out on the bed and climbed on top of her. He made sure not to bear any weight on her, but his lips never left hers, not until he pulled back to look into her eyes again.

"You're perfect, Sonia. You're so beautiful. I want to make love to you. I don't ever want to stop."

Perfect? She wasn't perfect. She was far from it. Fear washed suddenly over her, and she pushed Matthew away as hard as she could.

"No!" She leapt from the bed, her arms wrapped around her body trying to protect herself. "No, I can't do this."

"Sonia." Matthew reached out to her, and she could see the worry in his eyes. "Sonia, it is okay. I won't hurt you. We don't have to do anything you don't want to."

Sonia turned on her heels and fled into the bathroom. She locked the door behind her.

"Sonia, please. Talk to me."

"Look, give me half an hour. I want to shower and get dressed. Go and get us some breakfast."

"Sonia, that isn't going to happen. I am not leaving you."

"Matthew, please." She needed him to leave so she could think this through. "I promise you, I will be okay. I won't be able to calm down while I know you're out there." Or do what she had to do.

"Okay. I will go to a place nearby that does croissants and come straight back here. If you haven't opened the door by then, I will break it down."

"I will have. I promise."

Sonia heard the door close. She quickly scrambled to her feet and started to rifle through his shaving bag. He had an old-fashioned razor and she had never been so grateful. She pulled her PJ bottoms down. Her heart was beating so fast; it was like it was trying to escape her chest. She had gone six months without doing this. The first time had been just after she had been transferred to her fourth adoptive home. None of her foster parents could cope with her, she was a loose cannon after her mother's death. She could be sane and sensible one minute then climbing off the walls and smashing things the next. She got into fights and swore and shouted at her foster parents till they shipped her out to the next one and it all started again.

Scars littered her legs. This is why she could never have sex with Matthew. She was broken. She took the blade and brought it down on the biggest scar, breaking it open again. The pain surged through her veins, and she relaxed her head back against the wall as the blood dripped onto the floor. The rush of anxiety flowed away, and she went to her safe place and became the girl who had everything.

This time, the girl of her dreams had a man: Matthew. And she was allowing him to worship her body.

CHAPTER EIGHT

Matthew

Matthew tightly gripped the fence that surrounded the hotel. He tried to calm himself, but it was no use. He pulled his arm back, balled his fist and sent it smacking through the wooden panel, causing it to shatter and splinter all over the floor. He was a goddamn fool.

She was fragile; he had known that from the moment he had met her. For all her bravado, underneath she was delicate. Matthew had seen her files, never more than a year with one family until she was fifteen.

He had pushed her too far, too fast, too soon, and he needed to take a step back.

After leaving MI5, he had retreated into himself. The thought of having a relationship and having a woman depend on upon him for safety scared him. Even though he was fond of Amy, it was his job to look after her, and he was able to keep his feelings purely business. With Sonia, however, since the moment he had first met her, he wanted to look after her.

Matthew pushed off the fence and headed back to the hotel. He stood outside the door to their room for a few moments contemplating what he would find inside. He really didn't want to have to break the door down. As he placed his hand on the handle, it was shaking, and he took a deep breath and opened the door. Sonia was sitting on the bed, she was brushing her hair and pulling it back into a ponytail.

"I hope you like croissant and Danish."

"Sounds fantastic. I made our coffee."

"I hope mine is strong, it is going to be a long drive back."

"Two spoonfuls, just how you like it."

"Thank you."

Silence descended, and Sonia turned away. She fiddled nervously with her brush before placing it back into her bag. He watched her every movement. He had to say something, to show her everything was okay, but he couldn't. She turned and looked at him, and the edges of her eyes were red-rimmed from crying. "Please, I know you probably don't want to, but we need to talk about what happened."

Sonia lowered her head, "I'll see if I can get a flight back to England tomorrow."

"What?" He took a step closer to her, and she scrambled back. He held his hands up and went over to the desk and sat down on the chair. "Sonia, I am going to sit here, and I am not going to move, but you're going to talk to me. Why do you think that you would need to fly back to England?"

"Miss Jones can't have a bodyguard who suffers from panic attacks."

She was not telling him everything again. By rights, yes, if James knew of her having panic attacks, then he wouldn't want her to protect Amy.

"When was the last time you had an attack?"

"Sorry?" Clearly, Sonia hadn't expected that question.

"When was the last time that you had an attack?"

"Six months. "Sonia got to her feet, and she seemed to be walking a little gingerly. Maybe she had taken a bit of frustration out on the bath? He leant forward in his chair, his large hands resting on his open thighs. He kept his face blank, any emotion hidden away, but he gave off the aura that nobody was leaving the room till she spoke to him and he was satisfied with her answers. Sometimes he was glad for the Dom training that he and James had undertaken. Shame it didn't work though till he found Amy.

"Sonia, I am waiting for an answer."

"I can't remember."

"Try harder!" Even his voice was commanding.

"Matthew, please!"

"Was it because the person you were protecting was hurt?"

"No, I have never failed in my duty."

"Okay, was it because you were hurt?"

"No."

"What was it then!"

"I received a letter from my father." Sonia slapped her hands over her mouth as the words left it.

"You had an anxiety attack because your father sent you a letter? What was in it?"

"He sent me a visiting order."

"Did you visit him?"

"No. I tore the thing up and threw it in the bin. After I calmed down, I went to work."

"Did anything bad happen at work that day?"

"No, I seem to remember it being utterly boring. I followed my detail around the shops and stood beside her while she lunched in the Ivy."

"So nothing bad happened, and your panic attack was not related to the job?"

"No." Sonia looked down, her hands were twisted together in front of her.

"Then I will not be telling Mr North of what occurred here this morning."

"You would lose your job if Mr North were to find out."

"Mr North trusts my judgement, and Miss Jones will not be in harm's way. Your problems don't relate to the job."

"Matthew, please. I can't do this."

"No. Sit down Sonia, and I will have my say. You've had yours." She instantly sat on the edge of the bed, her eyes wide.

"When I was in MI5, I saw a colleague killed right before my eyes. She didn't have half the strength that you do, and it led to her downfall. She shouldn't have been in the position that she was, and that was my fault. That is why I don't talk about my time there: I am ashamed of it. And it is why I haven't had a relationship since then. I am not a saint, I got my kicks from women.

But you're different. I want a relationship with you. I want to protect you. I want to show you that you're a wonderful woman and worthy of so much more than you've been given in life. It won't be easy, we both have pasts which are dominating our present, but I think that together we can change our futures." Matthew took a deep breath as he finished his speech. He had never laid his heart on the table like that.

"Matthew." Tears filled her eyes and Matthew longed to be able to hold her in his arms and wipe them away, but he couldn't move. He needed her to take the first step. As if on cue, she got off the bed and dropped to her knees before him.

"There has only ever been one person that told me she loved me and that I was beautiful. My mother, it was her dying words to me. I am scared to hear you say them to me. I want to believe them. You're the first person to get me to admit what happened and make me feel good about myself. Since I started this job, I have never felt as happy as I do now. I feel like I belong. I have never had that before, and it is all happening so quickly for me. I feel like I am losing control and it puts me back there in that day. Everything going on around me, chaos, people everywhere. Matthew, what I am trying to say is I am scared to admit that...that I think I want a proper relationship with you as well."

Matthew let out the breath that he had been holding. He reached forward and dared to take her hands and pull them onto his lap. "I need to prove to you that I want you. That I am not going to reject you when you're a little bit of a brat or do something I don't like. We are going to take this slowly. Neither of us is ready for anything physical yet but, that doesn't mean that I will not want to put my arm around you and cuddle you if I have an opportunity. It also doesn't mean that I will not compliment you if you look lovely. A compliment that you'll take. And it certainly doesn't mean that I won't kiss you if I get the chance, in fact, there will be lots of that, but we will not go any further till we have revisited this discussion and we are both completely comfortable with it. Do you understand?"

"Do I get a say in this?" Matthew was sure he could hear a little chuckle in her voice. It lit up his heart.

"Right now, no, you don't." Matthew leant forward, he needed to kiss her, he needed to taste the sweetness of her lips again. They were like the best sugary treat he had ever had. "If you don't want to do something then you tell me 'red', yes?"

"Okay, Should I inform you that I am green, bordering on amber, at the moment?" This time, it was Matthew's turn to look shocked.

"You know what I want?"

"I have known since the moment I met you, Matthew."

He smiled, leant in, and pressed his lips to hers. She met them and hummed a moan of satisfaction into his mouth, and he could feel himself getting hard again. His poor cock had been rigid for most of the last twenty-four hours and without any chance of even being able to touch himself until he was safely tucked away in his room in the Maldives, it would just have to go on wanting what it couldn't have.

"Come on." Matthew stood and pulled Sonia in to nuzzle into his chest. "We need to get back to Bangalore."

CHAPTER NINE

Sonia

Sonia looked across the bed to the man sleeping with her. So much for taking things slowly. The night they arrived in the Maldives, Sonia decided she didn't want to be alone and tiptoed from her private cabin to Matthew's. She had expected him to be asleep, but he was sitting outside reading a book on his Kindle. He had been shocked to see her at first, but he put the Kindle down, pulled her into his arms, and then lead her to the bedroom where he tucked her in his bed and climbed in beside her. He kissed the top of her head, wrapped an arm around her, and within minutes, they were both asleep.

Sonia did the same every night after that.

It was hot, but she was still wearing her body-covering pyjamas. There was no way she could let Matthew know about what she had done in the bathroom when he had gone to get breakfast. Once it was healed, she would tell Matthew, and she would be able to say she did it in the past when she was in the foster homes. He would never need to know that in times of high stress it was the only way she could calm herself.

She didn't feel like she would need to do it again, she was relaxed and happy and enjoying herself. She was even starting to believe Matthew's comments about finding her beautiful and sexy. The fact that he seemed to get an erection every time he was near her helped. She wondered what it would feel like to have his cock in her mouth. Would he be delicious in his taste when she swallowed him? Her few forays into sex had been mostly blow jobs. She had discovered that getting a man off that way would satisfy him, and she wouldn't need to take her clothes off. God, she was pitiful. She was a twenty-five-year-old virgin. There she had said it. She had never had sex because she was scared that any man that went down there would call her a freak because she must be for harming herself. If Matthew really did love her enough, he wouldn't reject her. Would he? She hoped not. In the mean time, she had to be careful. Amy didn't need to cover her body, she was slender, muscular and wasn't covered in scars. She wandered around in just a skimpy bikini. Although James did still try to cover her up whenever the staff of the hotel appeared. Sonia was actually surprised Amy could sit down. She had seen James take her over his knee one time when she had refused to put her sarong on and spanked her backside. Sonia tried her hardest not to look, but she couldn't help but wonder what it felt like. It certainly wasn't painful or degrading in Amy's eyes. She was thoroughly enjoying it. When James had whispered into Amy's ear afterwards that she was so wet and had better get in the bedroom, Sonia had looked to Matthew and his eyes were dark with lust. He wasn't watching Amy and James though; he was completely focused on her. Sonia wondered what it would feel like to have his large hands punishing her that way. The wetness between her thighs told her all she needed to know, and she scurried off to the bathroom to relieve her sudden aching urge.

"Sonia!" Amy called out to her as she got off the boat. "Oh my God that was incredible. I got in the water and looked at the fish. You so have to do it!"

"I am sorry to have missed it. I drew the short straw." Matthew strode off the boat behind James. He winked at her.

Amy pouted at James. "Sonia should have been able to come with us."

"Next time. I will leave Matthew behind. He is far too moody anyway." James kissed Amy's nose as Matthew just grunted and hauled all the bags off the boat.

Sonia laughed as she took a bag from Matthew, and he

growled at her in reply. This time, it was Mr North's turn to laugh.

"Oh Amy, I think Matthew may have to punish Sonia the way I do you!" James patted her on the bottom.

"Fuck off, Boss!"

"Tetchy, Matthew."

"Mr North, I can assure you that Mr Carter has no right to punish me like that."

Matthew stood behind her, his erection pushing against her, and suddenly she felt a lot hotter. She coughed, and James burst into a fit of laughter.

"Yes, Sonia. I can see that if Matthew took you over his knee for your sarcasm, the first thing on your mind would be requesting an employee tribunal. Congratulations, Matthew. I am happy for you."

Sonia turned and looked up at Matthew. She wasn't ready to have people thinking that they were having sex. A relationship. Oh God. That was serious. She could feel her heart starting to beat faster, and she was getting hotter and hotter. Matthew stepped away from her and turned a frown face on James.

"We are good friends, boss. If it develops into a relationship, then I will let you know. Please don't tease either of us about it. It doesn't impact on the job that we do for you."

"Of course. Please accept my apologies."

"Of course," Matthew answered him, Sonia couldn't look up from the floor, she was beginning to feel sick.

"Sonia?" James' voice cut through everything.

"Sir, it isn't a problem. I will help Miss Jones back to the room with her belongings. I have placed some paperwork in Mr Carter's room that was faxed over for you to sign."

No more was said. Sonia held Amy's bag to her chest and followed her to her room while Matthew went off with James. By the time they entered the villa Amy and James' shared, Sonia was on the verge of tears. Amy walked straight over to the mini bar and pulled out a shot of brandy.

"Here, drink this. It will help."

"I am fine Amy." Sonia still couldn't look up and into the eyes of the woman she now thought of as her friend.

"I know you're not. Sonia, I know nothing of what is happening between you and Matthew but if it is something that you don't want to happen then you must tell me and I will have James put a stop to it."

"What?" Sonia panicked and looked straight at Amy. "No. I mean. I. We aren't sleeping together. Well, we are, but not sexually. Why is this so hard?"

Amy came straight up to her and wrapped her arms around her. "It doesn't have to be. Talk to me Sonia."

"Matthew and I have feelings for each other, but because of issues in both our pasts we are taking things slowly. I have spent the last few nights in his bed, but nothing has happened. I like him a lot, but I am not ready for more."

"I will talk to James and tell him to stop taunting you both."

"No, it's okay. James and Matthew are friends. It should be normal to tease each other."

"Not if it is going to upset you. Matthew will not want that."

"Amy?"

Her friend stepped away from her and took a seat on the bed. She patted for Sonia to come and sit beside her but Sonia chose to stay standing.

"Do you think that Matthew will want more from me now? How long will he wait?" Sonia almost felt like giggling, this was such a silly conversation for a twenty-five-year-old to have.

"He is a man, Sonia and he obviously thinks you're sexy." Sonia shook her head and screwed her face up a little bit. "As for how long he'll wait... I haven't known Matthew for long, but I think he'll wait for as long as you need."

"I think I could fall in love with him, but I am scared as to what that means."

"Physically or emotionally?"

"Both."

"Emotionally you'll deal with him. Come on, my relationship with James hasn't exactly been dull so far, but we get through it by keeping open lines of communication. Physically, well, what have you done so far?"

"We have kissed."

"And?"

"We have kissed." Sonia could feel herself blushing. She was sure she was actually sweating under this interrogation. "Okay. What have you done in the past?"

There was no way getting around this.

"I am a virgin. I have sucked a guy off before, but that's it."

"Okay, you can try that with Matthew. I am sure he would like that. Most men seem to if it is done right. What about letting Matthew touch you, get you off?"

She shook her head.

"Why?" Amy looked at her quizzically. It was as though she was an alien.

"I don't know. I can't explain it." It was all that came to her head at the time.

"Okay. James is into something called BDSM. It doesn't always involve sex. I am sure Matthew knows something about it as well. You could talk to him about that? You just need to learn to relax and trust each other."

Sonia spun on her heels. She needed some fresh air. This was all happening so fast. So much information in her head and the bloody cut on her leg kept tugging against her cheap polyester trousers causing her pain.

"I am sorry Amy; I need to get out of here. Sorry." Sonia sped out the door, Amy calling after her. He head was thumping and swirling, she could feel the sweat now dripping off her. All of a sudden she bent over and emptied the contents of her stomach onto the sand beneath her feet. What the hell was going on? She really didn't feel well. This was more than just embarrassment.

"Sonia." Matthew's voice called out. She looked up, and he

was standing there with James, a look of concern on his face. He took a step towards her, but all she could feel was herself falling. Her head hit the ground, pain shooting through her body as she blacked out.

CHAPTER TEN

Matthew

"Are you sure you're ready for this? She is different from the girls we have played with before." Matthew watched as James signed the papers and handed them back to him.

"As sure as you are that you're ready for marriage."

"Point taken. I won't interfere anymore. I like her, Amy likes her a lot as well. We both know that she has issues, and you aren't exactly Mr Sunshine, but I think you'll be good for each other. Just make sure Amy is the number one priority."

"You know I will always do my job!"

"Good. I want to get back to my girl. I think I have a couple more things I want to explore with her."

"I am surprised you both haven't got chafing!"

Matthew strode out of his villa with James in front of him.

"Jealous?"

"You maybe my boss but I don't think Amy would mind if I smacked you in the face for disrespect. We all know she wears the trousers now!"

Matthew turned his head and saw Sonia stumbling out of James and Amy's villa. She was deathly pale and shaking all over. She bent over and was violently sick everywhere.

"What the.... Sonia?" The last word was shouted out.

She looked up at him before she collapsed right in front of him. Matthew's legs were moving before his brain had even engaged. James was beside him as they both leapt over the small fence separating the villas. Amy ran out and straight to Sonia, but Matthew pulled Sonia into his arms.

"She is burning up." The unconscious form in his arms felt like fire.

"I will get a doctor. Take her to her room. Amy, help Matthew cool her down." James jumped up and sped towards the reception.

Matthew scooped Sonia up and ran towards his villa. Amy followed and turned the air conditioning up higher to cool the room. Matthew's head was scrambled. What was going on?

"What did you say to her?" He snapped at Amy.

"Just a little advice. Nothing to cause this. Matthew, this is a fever. We need to get her out of these clothes."

"I can't!"

"Then go and wait for James and the doctor because I am going to!" Amy didn't wait for Matthew, she tried to pull Sonia up to remove her jacket. She was struggling.

"I will hold her up." He took Sonia and held her still as Amy removed her jacket.

"Matthew, I am going to remove her shirt as well."

He nodded and averted his eyes. "Amy, tell her I didn't look."

"I will Matthew. Don't worry. Once she is cool, then she'll be all right."

"Thank you."

"You can lay her back down. Keep facing the other way. I am going to take her trousers off."

Matthew did so, and as Amy covered her top half with a sheet, he turned away. He wouldn't see her in the flesh until she agreed to it.

He waited till Amy said he could turn around, but all he heard was a loud gasp.

"Amy?"

Sonia must have woken up because he heard her scream.

"Get off me. Get out!"

"Sonia. You're awake? Are you okay!"

"Get out, both of you get out!"

"What?" Matthew wasn't keeping his back to her anymore; he turned around. She was huddled up and had pulled the sheet all around herself. She was still sweating, but this time, she was paler. "Amy?"

Sonia was looking straight at her friend; Matthew could see the absolute terror in her eyes. Amy was moving her mouth, but nothing seemed to be coming out. The door opened behind them, and James and a doctor ran in.

"Miss Anderson?"

Matthew pointed to Sonia.

"I understand you fainted, and Mr North tells me you've a fever. Can I take a look?"

"No!" Sonia scrambled further up the bed. "I got hot. It is hot out today, that's all. I feel much better. Please, an hour's rest and I will be all right."

"You won't." Amy whispered the words, but Matthew heard them.

"Amy, what is going on?" James came to Amy's side and wrapped his arms around her.

"Sonia, I have to tell them."

Sonia was crying now.

"What is going on?" He shouted and thumped his fist down on a nearby cupboard. Sonia startled and turned her head to him. "Show me?"

She didn't say anything, just let the sheet fall. Her eyes went blank. Matthew looked down to her legs. Criss-crossed patterns of scars rose from both her thighs. One of them looked red and angry. It was new. And it was infected. Matthew's mouth went dry.

Pondicherry. The bathroom. It all hit him. He left her, and she had cut herself. He stumbled backwards, bumping into the wall and sliding down it. Sonia shut her eyes and let the tears fall.

"Amy." James' voice cut through the silence. "The doctor will see to Sonia. Come on. We should go back to our room and let him work." Matthew watched them both leave. He got to his feet as the doctor came over to Sonia.

"Was the razor blade clean Ma'am?"

"It wasn't sterile." She looked over to him, "Mr Carter had used it for shaving." The bottom fell out of his world.

She had used his razor.

The doctor placed a thermometer into Sonia's ear. "Your temperature isn't as bad as I expected it to be. I suspect the heat contributed to your fainting. You do have an infection, though. I will clean up the cut and give you a shot of antibiotics. When do you leave?"

"Tomorrow."

"You should be fit to fly. I will come and check on you before you do. When you return home, you must go straight to a doctor and get it checked again. Ma'am-- you need to look at counselling as well. That is important."

"I have a counsellor."

"Mr Carter, you're responsible for this woman?"

Matthew was listening to the conversation but struggling to take everything in.

"Yes, I am."

"She'll need rest and plenty of fluids today. Try to keep her cool but don't use cold water on her. It can do more harm than good."

"I will."

They sat in silence as the doctor did his work. When he was finished, Matthew placed the sheet over Sonia and followed the doctor out.

"Will she heal?"

"She has lots of old scars. She has been doing this for a long time. The one she opened is probably her 'go to' cut. The one she uses when desperate. Do you know why she did it?"

"I have a good idea."

"Talk to her about it. It is all you can do, at the moment."

"Thank you, doctor."

"If she gets worse, call me. I will sort the bill with Mr North."

Matthew nodded and went back inside.

"Sonia." She looked over at him. "Start explaining."

"Should I go back to my room?"

"You even go try to go back to your room, and I will tie

you to that bed, and we will remain here till you decide to talk!"

She made sure the sheets covered every inch of her body. "I cut myself. I have done it since I'was a kid. I am a freak. Don't worry, I know what you're going to say."

"How do you know what I am going to say?"

"Because I have heard it all before."

Matthew pursed his lips together. He grabbed the end of the sheet and pulled it off her.

"Matthew!"

"Quiet. You don't have permission to speak. You'll listen to me."

"I don't have permission to speak?"

"Silence, or I will put you over my knee and spank that beautiful little arse till you can't lay on your front or back. I have seen the way you watch James do it to Amy. I know that every time you do, you disappear to get yourself off."

She didn't say anything, just made herself small like she was trying to hide.

"You were passed between different foster homes, told you were a troublemaker, and you believe it. It caused you to feel pain, so you decided to start cutting yourself to get a pain of a different kind. Am I right?"

"Yes." Her voice was mouse-like in reply.

"You're not well enough now for me to show you a different way of releasing pain when you're stressed, but when we return to England and the doctor has given you all clear I will be showing you. And Sonia, don't think I mean that I will have sex with you. I will not do that till I believe you're ready for it and you agree." It suddenly hit him, of course, it made complete sense. "You're a virgin."

Sonia whimpered and placed her head in her hands.

"Yes."

Matthew couldn't help but feel a little bit excited by that thought; he would be the first one to be with her.

"Okay we will discuss correcting that when you're better. I have to show you what you've been missing out on."

"Matthew, you don't have to do this."

He let out a gravelly breath. He was at the end of his tether with her self-deprecation.

"Lay back on the bed!" The commanding tone was back, and though Sonia hesitated at first, she did as commanded. Matthew pulled his shirt over his head and climbed next to her on the bed.

"Don't move." She swallowed down a gulp as Matthew brought his lips down to hers. She was the best taste he had ever had. Slowly he moved his mouth over her jaw, down the slender column of her neck and across her shoulder blade. He lowered her bra strap and pulled her right breast out of her bra. Her nipples were the perfect mix of pink and brown. He pinched the tip, and she moaned.

"Pain can also be pleasurable. Remember red if you want me to stop."

She nodded at him.

"I need to hear that you understand Sonia."

"Yes, Sir."

"Good girl."

He lowered his mouth again, travelling down her body, savouring every inch of her flesh. He stopped at her thighs and looked back up at her. Sonia's eyes were wide.

"Every inch of you is beautiful." And he pressed delicate kisses to her scars. He put his nose against the delicate fabric of her pants and took a long inhalation. He carefully pulled her pants down. She was completely shaved. His cock leapt.

He parted her labia and ran a finger down from her clit to the entrance of her moist pussy. She instinctively shut her legs.

"I know you've brought yourself to orgasm before. This will be no different, just more intense."

She opened her thighs, and he traced his finger over her again. This time, he tested her entrance and pushed a finger slowly in. She was so tight. He circled his thumb over her clit, teasing the sensitive nub from its hood. She was fantastic. Her breath quickened. He flicked his finger over her clit again as he pressed another finger inside her and bent his head to kiss the scars on her legs again. She arched her back and exploded around him. Her pussy clamped down on his fingers as she rode her waves of pleasure.

He was her salvation, and she would be his. In that instant he knew it.

As she came down from her climax, Matthew withdrew his fingers and brought them to his mouth. She tasted so sweet, just a hint of tanginess. He pulled her knickers back up and corrected her bra. Sonia was exhausted; the fever and the orgasm had wiped her out. He placed the sheet over her. And sat beside her on the bed as she settled herself and closed her eyes.

She drifted to sleep, and Matthew stayed by her side.

◆

CHAPTER ELEVEN

Sonia

Three months later.......

"How was he today?" Sonia entered the bedroom that she now shared with Matthew and placed her bag down on the oak table.

"He managed to shave this morning and then locked himself in his office to work. I took him a tray of food, but when I went back an hour later to collect it, he had only taken a little bite of the sandwich." Matthew replied to her as he lay on the bed, his arms propped behind his head. The look of boredom on his face told Sonia everything she needed to know. Ever since Amy had left James, Matthew had become increasingly frustrated with his job. It had taken a month before James even left his bed after he was shot, and he still wasn't the same man. Sonia and Matthew had discussed finding Amy and talking to her, but they agreed it was probably best to leave them to sort out everything for themselves.

"Miranda is anxious about him. She was quiet when we were shopping."

"I know. Sophie should be here later today, so hopefully, that will help. He always seems to brighten up when his sister is around."

"I hope so. Do you want to watch over Miranda tomorrow, and I will stay at home with James?" When Amy had left, Sonia had been assigned to protect Mrs North instead. She suspected it was James' way of making sure she still had something to do. "I can't promise you it will be a thrilling engagement, but she does have the talk at the art museum tomorrow. Some of the attendees always make me chuckle."

"No, I will stick with James. I will try and force him into the office tomorrow for an hour or so. At least that will get him out. I am sure I can make up some excuse to get him there."

Sonia removed her trousers and placed them in the linen basket that she had brought to try and tidy up Matthew's room a little bit. For such a disciplined man, he had a terrible habit of leaving his worn underpants on the floor. She reached for a pair of yoga pants. "Are you forgetting the rules?"

Sonia stopped with half a leg into the pants. "Sorry?"

"We are alone in our rooms."

"Your body and your soul are both beautiful. When we are alone you know you're not supposed to wear clothes so you can realise that."

"I thought you would want dinner."

"Depends on what you're serving?" His voice turned gravelly and dominant.

She stepped back out of the pants and placed them on the side, her shirt, bra and knickers joined them.

"That is much better. Come here." He moved to the end of the bed and opened his legs wide as he beckoned her.

Sonia couldn't argue with that look, when his eyes went dark, and he looked at her like she was a delicious dessert to savour.

She came between his legs and he pressed his head against her breasts. He didn't move. She could just hear him inhaling her scent, and feel his warm breath against her tender flesh. He pulled back and ran a hand over the healing scars on her leg and dropped a kiss on them before letting out a long sigh.

"He is dying on the inside. I don't know what to do to save him. I feel useless."

"You're doing all you can. Mr North and Amy just need time. We will give them another few months, and then we will spur them along a little bit." Sonia got down on her knees and leant her head into his lap. He stroked her hair, his thick digits running through the soft tendrils.

"I love you, Sonia. Don't ever leave me."

"I have no plans to, Matthew. Who else will, or even could, make me feel beautiful like you do?"

"Are you doubting again?"

She shook her head. " I know what happens when I do. Although maybe...."

"Deliberate antagonism doesn't get you a spanking, my dove."

"Why a dove?" She looked at him with a querying expression

"Because you're learning to fly."

She liked that idea.

"Matthew, Sonia." A knock and Miranda's voice at the door.

"Get on the bed and in position. I will be back in a minute."

Sonia jumped eagerly onto the bed as Matthew disappeared. She listened to the voices coming from the hall.

"I am sorry to disturb you. Sophie and Grayson are here already. His bodyguard is asking for you, and James won't come out of his office. Can you help?"

"Of course. Give us five minutes, and we will both be there."

"Thank you, Matthew."

"No worries, Mrs North."

Sonia got off the bed and put her clothes back on as Matthew returned to the room.

"You heard everything then?"

"Yes. Why won't he come out of his office?"

"I don't know."

Sonia grabbed her navy jacket off the side as Matthew swapped his Led Zeppelin t-shirt and jeans for a formal suit.

"Do you want me to deal with Grayson's security detail, while you sort James?"

They left their rooms together and headed down to the main section of the house in Knightsbridge.

"I better sort them. His bodyguard is a good man, but he can be a bit self-important. You go in and meet Sophie. You'll like her."

"Okay. Call if you need me."

Sonia went to walk around the corner to the lounge, but Matthew grabbed her arm, her back landed against the wall as his body pressed against her and he drew a kiss from her lips.

"Matthew Carter. You have a girlfriend?" The excited shriek came from behind them and they jumped apart. Matthew grunted out a cough as Sonia flushed.

"Miss Sophie. May I introduce Sonia? She is your mother's bodyguard."

Sonia raised her head and smiled as a woman jumped towards them and threw her arms around Matthew, first, and then Sonia.

"Oh, my God. Come tell me all about yourself. How long have you been together?"

Sophie linked arms with her and dragged her into the sitting room. Matthew winked a goodbye and headed off towards James' office.

"Sophie, leave the poor girl alone." Miranda rolled her eyes as they entered.

"How can I, mum? I mean, Matthew has a girlfriend. Sit, Sonia."

A man with long black hair and American-Indian features came into view.

"Sophie." His gravelly voice sounded just like Matthew's was when he was in dominant mode. "Come sit with me, and you can question Miss Anderson without making her feel like it is an interrogation."

"You're no fun." Sophie pouted at the man Sonia surmised was her fiancé.

"Put your bottom lip away and sit or I will show you just how much fun I can be."

"Will you spank me?"

"Sophie, please." Sonia was sure Miranda turned green.

"There are things a mother doesn't need to know."

"Sorry mum." Sophie finally sat down next to her fiancé, and he wrapped a protective arm around her shoulder.

"Miss Anderson. I am Grayson Moore, Miss North's fiancé. It is a pleasure to meet you. Miranda has been telling us about how you've become a valued member of the protection team. How long have you been here now?"

"Only six months."

"You helped rescue Mrs North when she was taken?"

"I did."

"Thank you on Sophie's part for that."

Sonia found it a little strange that Sophie was no longer speaking and Grayson was dictating the conversation. She was sure she could say thank you on her own.

"I am just sorry that I couldn't prevent Mr. North getting shot as well."

"It was a difficult situation." Sophie squirmed beside the imposing man. "You may ask your questions now Sophie."

"Thank you." She winked at him and turned her head to Sonia.

"Is it true you're dating Matthew?"

"I am, yes."

"Oh, I am so happy." She brought her hands to her face in a joyful prayer.

"We are taking our relationship slowly. Mr. North isn't doing too well." Maybe she could divert the attention away from her.

"He needs to just get out and have a night in the club. That will sort him." Grayson tried to mumble under his voice.

"Club?"

"I don't need more babysitting. I just need to catch up on all the fucking work I have missed while I was in the hospital." James' angry voice shattered through the door before Grayson had a chance to answer her question.

"She is your sister, and you'll get your arse in there and say hello, or I will smack you in the face till you pass out and I can drag you in there."

"You know you aren't so indispensable that I can't fire you."

"I am. Nobody else would put up with your shit."

'Go fuck your girlfriend before she walks out on you like mine did."

"I will let that one go. Now get the fuck in there!"

The door opened, James stumbled in, and Matthew blocked the exit.

"There is the welcoming brother I know and love." Sophie stood and held her arms open to him.

"You didn't have to come, Sophie. I am fine, I just have lots of work to catch up on." James made no effort to embrace his sister. He stood with his arms folded and glared at everyone in the room.

"You're a mess, stop lying to us and yourself."

"The woman I love left me. Sorry, I am not a happy clown at the moment."

Sonia was getting scared.

"You lied to her. She needs time to calm down, and then you can talk to her."

"I didn't lie."

"You did!"

"I was protecting her!"

Sonia looked over to Matthew and could see how much this was hurting him. James was his best friend as well as his boss, and there was nothing he could do for him. She coughed, and they all looked at her. "Mr North, if I may, Miss Jones loves you, she just needs time to understand what happened. She used her safe word--that doesn't mean she's finished with you. Matthew taught me that it means a break for reflection and understanding."

Sonia looked back over to the figure that loomed large in the doorway. Matthew had an adoring smirk on his face. It made her heart leap.

"Miss Anderson is right," Grayson spoke next, and everyone turned their heads to him. "Matthew, how far is my club from here?"

"Half an hour, sir."

"Miss Anderson is trained?" Grayson raised an eyebrow as he spoke. Why did he need to know if she was trained? She was a bodyguard. Of course, she was trained!

"She is learning."

"Sophie, take Miss Anderson and help her dress. You as well. Wear my favourite outfit. Mr Carter will send any requirements he has to you both shortly. James, Matthew, both of you get changed as well. I think a long shower is required for you, James."

"I am not going to the club!" James folded his arms across his chest as Sophie got up and came over to Sonia.

While the men continued to argue, Sonia leant in and whispered to Sophie.

"Why are we going to a club? Are we going to try and find James another woman?"

"Nothing of the sort. Gray asked about you being trained?"

"Yes, I am a bodyguard. I had training."

"Not that sort of training."

"What sort then?"

"BDSM. I have a feeling my fiancé wants to remind my brother of the rules of being a dominant lover."

"Miss North? How will this help Mr North?"

"Please, call me Sophie. We all have issues that we keep inside." She looked towards the men as James finally and very reluctantly agreed. Matthew allowed him out of the room to change. "It takes a certain knowledge to find it and help guide someone to overcome it. That doesn't only work between Dom and submissive. It works on all levels."

CHAPTER TWELVE

Matthew

Matthew pulled Sonia closer as they walked into the club. She may not be collared, but she was his, and nobody was going to get close to her. James went straight to the bar and ordered a large whisky. The two-drink rule was going to be a problem later on.

James had made it clear he was not here to play and as soon as Matthew and Grayson disappeared into rooms, he was out of there. Matthew wasn't entirely aware of what Grayson was trying to do; he just hoped he did it quickly and that it worked.

Matthew took a seat on a plush, black leather sofa and motioned for Sonia to sit beside him. She hadn't spoken since they entered the club, but her eyes had been flickering between various scenes that were going on around them. Sophie took a seat at Grayson's feet.

"So, what are you planning? He won't scene."

"He might not have a choice." Matthew wasn't sure he liked the look that crossed Grayson's face.

"Sophie. While I talk with Matthew and James, why don't you take Sonia and show her around? Stay with her at all times. If she gets into any trouble, your punishment will be denial. Do you understand?"

"Yes, Master."

"Do you want to go, Sonia?"

"I would like to look." She bowed her head as he took her hands. She raised her eyes up from under her long lashes. He slid his hand under one of the slashes in the sleeveless top she had on. The top was covered in them and gave an illusion to her breasts being covered. In fact, if she moved in the wrong way anybody would be able to see them as she had no bra on. Her nipples were hard already as he alternately took them in his hand and twisted.

"Stay close to Sophie. You don't have permission to speak except to her."

He removed his hand, and she whimpered from the lost contact.

"Yes, Master."

Matthew watched them walk away.

"When are you going to let me in on the plan? Especially since it seems to involve my property."

"Have you whipped her before? I appeal to remember that's your forte."

He had, a few times. She enjoyed it.

"Yes."

Grayson shook his head, and James took a seat near them.

"Your club's rules are shit. Tell them I want another drink."

"The two-drink maximum is for everyone's protection. There are no exceptions to the rules."

"I might as well go home then."

"You'll stay. We are just starting the evening."

From behind them, a commotion started up. Several women screamed, and a loud thud echoed around the vaulted ceiling. It was the direction Sophie and Sonia had headed in. Matthew jumped to his feet; Grayson stood a little more casually. James didn't move at all.

A muscular man dressed in only a leather loincloth rushed over to them.

"Master Grayson. Master Noah needs you at once."

"Of course. James, Matthew, would you care to join me? I suspect I need to officiate something. I could use your input."

Matthew stomach sank. He clenched his fists because he was very close to smashing them into Grayson's face. He followed Grayson, and as the sea of observers parted he saw Sonia being held back by Noah from a Dom that was laid flat out on the floor. He rushed over to her and pulled her away.

"Hands off her."

"Is she yours?" Noah said as he bent down to assist the beleaguered Dom up from the floor.

"She is."

"Is she not collared?"

"Not yet!" Matthew gritted his teeth as he searched Sonia for signs of injury or distress.

"She shouldn't have been left alone, then." The man who had been on the floor brushed himself down as he spoke. Matthew glared at him as he turned his attention to Sonia.

"What happened?"

"I was watching a couple on a cross, and he started speaking to me. I couldn't answer him, as you said I couldn't talk. I didn't want to disobey you. I turned to Sophie to get her to talk to him, but she was talking to someone else. When I did, he tried to grab me. My instincts kicked in, and I flipped him onto the floor. I am sorry. I didn't know what else to do."

"Shush. It is okay." He pulled her into his chest in comfort.

"How was I supposed to know she couldn't speak? She wasn't collared and was standing alone. This isn't my fault. When I touched her, she should have dropped to the floor. I demand punishment for her." The man turned to Grayson. "You have rules here, after all."

It suddenly dawned on Matthew what was going on. Grayson had set this all up.

"Not happening!" He wrapped his arms around the shivering woman nestled against him.

"Master Grayson, if he is her Dom and doesn't allow the punishment, then I want his membership revoked."

"Revoke it?" Whatever game Grayson had in his mind, Matthew was playing along correctly, judging by the smirk on the owner's face.

"I don't think I can do that. After all, his employer requires it for his job." Everyone turned to look at James who was casually leaning against a spanking horse.

"Doesn't bother me. Not if it means I can go home."

"But what about when you need to bring clients here, James? Your bodyguard wouldn't be able to carry out his job."

"Just do it Matthew, and then we can go home." James let out a frustrated moan. Sonia clinched harder to Matthew's chest.

"I am sorry, Sir, but I will not punish my woman for something that's my fault."

"It would seem we have a stalemate then. No one will be leaving anytime soon. Not until we can sort this out. I suggest we all take a seat and allow others to continue their scenes."

Sonia lifted her head and looked straight into Matthew's eyes. Her dark eyes were watery with unshed tears. Matthew shook his head again.

"Oh, for fuck's sake. What punishment do you want? I will do it." James stepped forward and spoke to the man that had been wronged. So this was Grayson's game.

"I think ten lashes with a bullwhip. James, you've trained on them?"

Matthew clenched his fists. He wasn't sure he could watch this, let it happen.

"Yes, I have. Matthew, put Sonia over the bench."

"Are you not going to ask my permission to do this?" Matthew asked.

"Do I need it?"

Matthew met Sonia's eyes and leant to whisper in her ear.

"Sonia, you can use your safe word at any time if you don't want to do this."

"Can you stay with me?"

"I am going nowhere. You're going to need to remove your clothes."

"People will see..."

"At this moment, no woman in this room can match you."

Matthew kept Sonia as close as possible and helped her remove her top and trousers. Small gasps came from the crowd when they saw the marks on her legs.

"At least no one is looking at my breasts or vagina." She let out a little giggle before looking down at the floor. Matthew led her over to the bench and placed her so her back was facing James, who already had the flogger in hand, twisting it in practice.

"Keep your eyes focused on me. James will want you to count. I will help you. It will be a bit more painful than we have used before, and he doesn't know your body as I do but..."

"It is okay." She interrupted him. "I am ready," Sonia spoke to Grayson but kept her eyes on his.

Grayson addressed the crowd, " Miss Anderson has consented to punishment for disrespecting a Master. She'll be given ten lashes by Master James. Master Noah, you speak for this gentleman. Does he accept the punishment?

"Yes, he does."

"You may begin then." Grayson nodded to James who pulled his arm back.

"Maybe you should think that she is Amy." Sophie spoke just as James started to bring the flogger down. The world seemed to turn in slow motion to Matthew as he saw James stop his movement. The recognition dawning on James' face as the tendrils fell gently onto Sonia's back. Her eyes went wide. He was around the side of the bench, and she was in his arms before the flogger even hit the floor. James sagged to the ground. Sophie wrapped her arms around him as Grayson stood over them.

"Matthew, take Sonia to my private room upstairs. Noah, let him in please. Anything they want ensure they have it. We will look after James."

Matthew could hear his heart almost beating out of his chest as the adrenaline flooded him. Noah led them away.

"They broke him." She whispered so softly that Matthew barely heard it.

"He'll be better now."

"Did you know what the plan was?"

"I guessed it the second I saw the Dom on the floor."

The door to a velvety, plush room was opened. A king-size bed lay in the middle, and mirrors adorned several of the walls and ceiling. Grayson had good taste. Matthew set Sonia on the bed and tucked her into the Egyptian cotton bedding to keep her warm. He went back to the door to talk to Noah.

"How did you get the Dom to agree to that?"

"He owed Grayson. He didn't have much choice. Your woman has good moves."

"Don't get any ideas."

"Grayson says you can have the room for the night. He has men outside to watch the family. You won't be disturbed. Ring if you need anything."

"Thanks, Noah." Matthew shut the door on the outside world. It was just him and Sonia alone together in the room. He sat on the bed, and she reached out to him. He couldn't help but stare at her.

"What? Do I have something on my face?"

"Sorry. I can't believe you didn't use your safe word."

"I didn't need to. I knew that you would take me out of there if it meant I would be hurt."

"That flogger isn't a lightweight one."

"Show me?"

"Don't be silly."

"I am not." She dropped the sheet, and it pooled around her knees as she knelt on the bed with her seductive curves displayed. "When I removed my clothes, I thought of how horrible my scars looked."

"You did?" He raised his eyebrow. "Well, that does deserve some sort of punishment."

"Please, Master."

"Bend over, Sonia. It is time to play."

CHAPTER THIRTEEN

Sonia

Sonia had managed to hide the trembling in her hands the entire time, but now she was alone with Matthew she didn't have to. As she knelt before him naked, it wasn't fear causing her shivers but more the anticipation of what was to come. He had used soft floggers on her before. The sight of the one that James had held up had sent an electric pulse of desire down her spine.

"Sonia, I am not going to use the one James was about to employ on you. I am not prepared to go that far yet. What I will use though will leave marks. Are you sure you're ready for that?"

She nodded.

"I need to hear you say it."

"I am ready, Master."

"Good girl."

"Would you've stopped James if he went to hit me?"

"He isn't just my boss, Sonia, he is also my closest friend. I want nothing more than for him to be back to the man that he was rather than the shell he has been the last few months but there are limits. I had to let Grayson's little plan run its course as much as I could. But I promise you. James North Wouldn't have left a mark on your skin. That is my job. I don't share my responsibilities when it comes to you.

"I think I like that answer." And she did. Matthew broke her from her thoughts with a kiss to her forehead, stopping her in front of a wall that contained a St. Andrew's cross.

"I am going to strap you to this. How are you feeling?"

Sonia looked at the strange contraption. "Green."

"Place your arms in the loops, and I'll secure you."

Sonia did as instructed. Matthew wrapped the soft leather cuffs around her wrists and ankles. This was a little nerve-wracking, but excitement was also beginning to build, a heat coiling within her. She couldn't see what Matthew was doing, but she could hear him remove his jacket and shirt. Suddenly his fiery breath was on the back of her neck, and the hairs on her arms stood like a salute to their master.

"I am going to use a knotted flogger on you. It will leave marks, but I'll take care of you after. Ten, for doubting your beauty again. I want you to count. I need you to stay with me."

"I'll count."

"Pardon?" Matthew's brought his large hand down hard on her pert backside, the reverberation of lust pulsed through her.

"I'll count, Master." Her answer was breathless.

His closeness was gone. She heard the swish through the air and when the pain exploded over her buttocks she realised he already had his tool of choice in his hand.

"One."

"Louder. I need to be able to hear you clearly." The knotted tendrils came down again.

"Two."

"Do you understand you're being punished because you doubted your beauty?" The leather met her flesh twice more in quick succession as he spoke.

"Three. Four. You tell me I am beautiful, and I shouldn't doubt your judgement."

The next four lashes came with only the count spoken between them. Sonia's mind was fading into the realm of pain and the oh-so-beautiful pleasure she was feeling, but her consciousness of the number brought her back. The heat of her arousal pooled between her legs and the tender spot between her legs ached for his touch. This was more intense than any of the previous play they had engaged in. The final lash came down, and as she screamed out ten, she heard the flogger drop to the floor, and Matthew's lips met her inflamed skin. He trailed lower, caressing her body. He massaged her buttocks.

He dipped two fingers inside her and angled the rest to circle the engorged nub of her sex. Within seconds, she was screaming out his name as she came in an explosion. As she slowly came down from her high, Matthew withdrew his hand and eased her into his arms as he undid the cuffs binding her to the cross. He laid her out on the bed on her stomach and reached over to the bedside table to take a bottle of oil. Silently he smoothed it into her body. She let out a moan of contentment as he returned the bottle to the table.

"How are you feeling?"

"Like I am floating. I found it so hard to count. I just wanted to drift away."

"Subspace."

Sonia turned onto her side to face Matthew.

""Do you want me to help you dress so I can take you home?"

Sonia opened her eyes wide and looked at Matthew in confusion.

"Home?"

"Yes. It is where we live. Big House, Knightsbridge address. Owned by a grumpy boss."

"But I thought?"

Matthew got up from the bed, Sonia couldn't help but notice the rather visible bulge in his leather trousers.

"It is too soon."

Sonia sat up, her bottom smarting a little as she did so.

"Too soon. But earlier you said you were going to take my virginity? What has changed?" There was an angry tone to her voice. She couldn't understand why not more than half an hour ago he wanted to sleep with her but now he didn't. Maybe she wasn't what he wanted? But then the tent in his pants? It was probably just the flogging that turned him on, not Sonia herself. Matthew turned away towards the door.

"I'll wait outside."

"Don't bother. I'll get a taxi back.

Before she could collect the rest of her clothes, she was thrown back against the wall, one of Matthew's large hands massaging a naked breast. His erection grinding into her still thigh as he growled.

"Is that what you think? I want to go out there and fuck someone else?"

"Well, you won't fuck me despite promising. I obviously did something wrong." She turned her head away as he tried to kiss her. She wanted nothing more than to kick him in that hard swelling inching closer to the cleft between her legs but her stupid body betrayed her as the moisture of her arousal started to flow again. He twisted her around and landed a hard smack on her inflamed skin.

"I told you never to doubt yourself. Doubt again, and I'll tan this rosy rear so that you really won't be able to sit tomorrow. I want you so much, but I don't want to hurt you. I don't make love. I fuck. I can't guarantee that I won't hurt you and that scares the shit out of me!"

She didn't know where it came from, but she let out a little laugh. He smacked her arse again.

"I don't think that's funny."

"I don't either." She tried to shift in his arms, but he was holding her too tight. "I don't want tender love-making Matthew. I want you to fuck me till I am raw and marked as only yours."

"I can't do it. I can't hurt you on your first time."

"Unless I have a first time, you'll never be able to fuck me."

"I am scared I'll break you."

"You saved me, you can never break me."

Sonia dropped to her knees before him as she spoke.

"Please Master, may I suck you?"

"What?" He looked up from whatever point he had been studying on the floor.

"You won't fuck me, but I won't leave you like this." She placed her hand over the tented trousers. "Please."

He nodded his head in agreement, and Sonia reached to undo his belt. Slowly she moved onto the buttons and undid them before lowering his trousers to the floor. She slipped her hand under the cotton of his tight boxer shorts and freed his cock. It was the first time she had seen it. Everything they had done in the past had been for her. It was a beautiful length and certainly wide. The purple crown stood proudly searching for a much-needed relief. She leant in and licked the tip of her tongue up the shaft.

It was salty to taste, she murmured her delight to finally give him pleasure. Matthew placed his hand on her head. "Flick over the head and back down to my balls. I love my balls being sucked."

Sonia did as he asked. She took one at a time into her mouth, and he groaned. "Oh God. Your mouth was made for this. For doing this to me. Take my cock in."

She opened her mouth wide, and slowly, she brought him as far in as she could. He touched the back of her throat, and she gagged a little.

"We can work up to that, my little dove. For now, just be comfortable. It still feels like heaven for me." That gave her confidence, and she began to move up and down his rigid length.

"Play with my balls."

She obeyed cupping the sensitive jewels.

"Yes, oh yes. That's it." His hand tangled into her hair as he started to lose himself to the feeling. He was controlling her pace now but never pushed her further than she could go. Perspiration beaded on his head.

"I am going to come. Pull back if you don't want to take it."

Sonia made no move other than to continue her assault on his cock.

The first spurt hit the back of her throat, and she watched as he thrust his head back and closed his eyes in ecstasy. She swallowed as much of him down as she could. When he was finished, she released him with a pop and he sunk to his knees beside her.

"That was. That was the best feeling ever."

Sonia secretly felt very proud of herself, but she needed to follow through on the second part of her plan.

"Matthew, take me now, please."

CHAPTER FOURTEEN

Matthew

Those words, that plea, the eyes staring at him full of longing. How could he deny her what she wanted? He flipped her onto her back and thrust straight in. So wet, so tight, she was constricting him like a vice. Sonia cried out as he pierced the barrier to her purity.

Shit.

What was he doing?

Not like this.

He withdrew quickly and threw himself away from the bed. His head banging against the wall in rhythm with his curses. Fuck, Fuck, Fuck. He should leave. He should get out right now. He couldn't look at her.

"I'm sorry." Sonia's voice finally broke the air of tension in the room.

"You're sorry?" He looked up at her.

"It was only a moment of pain. I shouldn't have cried out like that."

"Don't you apologise for what happened. That was completely my fault."

"But I asked you to do it."

"And I should have done it better; taken my time; been gentle."

"Matthew, I don't want careful. I want you, not what you think you should be to me. I'm a big girl now." She smiled at him. "I can handle it, and if I can't then I'll tell you."

"Trust."

"Trust. Now, where were we." He let go of her chin, and she reached out to touch his now deflated cock. It thickened instantly.

"I need to stop letting lower brain take over."

"No, the exact opposite. Switch your brain off and let him do what he needs to do."

He raised an eyebrow at her and watched her melt into the bed with desire. "Lay down."

She gripped the cotton sheet. Her legs parted, giving him a view of her sex, already flushed and glistening for him. He stood before her and stroked the full length of cock, working from the tip all the way to the trunk that joined to the rest of his body. He bent and pulled a condom from the pocket of his trousers. She watched him tear it open with his teeth and cover his massive length.

Placing himself at her entrance, he risked a look at her face. Her fists were scrunched so tight he could see the whites of her knuckles.

"Matthew?" The words were breathless and pleading. Taking his time, he pushed slowly inside her again. Her heat was a welcoming cocoon with each inch that he pressed in. Finally, he was in to the hilt. He stilled, waiting for her to adjust to his size.

"So full. Move. Please." Her head fell back against the pillow, and she let out a long moan that reverberated through her body to his cock.

He leant forward and brought his mouth to hers, their lips and tongues tangling together at a frenzied pace. He was lost in her. Sweetly innocent but the vibrant tang of hunger invaded his nostrils adding to the blood pumping rapidly around his body and into his dick. He quickened his pace while moving his mouth over the line of her chin, nibbling his way down her neck, across her collarbone and to her breasts. The small peaks were hard, and he flicked at one with his tongue, before sinking his teeth into the deep red nipple.

"Fuck." His balls tightened.

She dug her nails deep into his skin when he shifted and hit the tender spot inside her. He bit down on her shoulder, his teeth sinking into the tender flesh marking her as his and his alone.

"Get there Sonia, touch yourself. I can't hold on much longer."

He felt her tiny fingers slide between them and stroke her clit. He quickened his pace. His balls slapped against her arse with every thrust.

He met her eyes. She flew over the edge; he watched her. It wasn't until the last second that she rolled her eyes back in her head, shuddering all around him. It was all he needed, and he followed her over. Growling out her name while filling the condom to bursting point. He could barely breathe. His heart beat so fast that he could hear it ringing in his ears. She whimpered when he gently withdrew. With wobbly legs he got to his feet, tied off the condom, and threw it into his bag on the floor. He would dispose of it later. There was a bin for that sort of stuff, but he'd never left his DNA behind. Force of habit from the job.

In the corner of the room stood a sink and fresh towels. He turned the water on, tested its temperature and wetted the cloth. Sonia still laid on the bed, her chest lifting and falling rapidly trying to catch her breath. He wiped her clean. This room was equipped for most eventualities, and he took some ice from the fridge's freezer and wrapped it in a fresh towel. Tenderly he placed it between her legs, but she winced.

"Keep it there for a while. It will help with the discomfort."

He climbed into the bed next to her and lay her gently out on his chest.

"Thank you." She murmured, half awake, half asleep.

"What for?"

"The best night of my life."

"I think I should be thanking you. You talked me down this time."

A knock at the door. He pulled the sheets over them.

"Yes."

It opened slightly, and Sophie stuck her head in.

"Sorry to disturb you Master Matthew but James wishes

to return home soon. Do you want Master Grayson to see if he can allocate one of his guards to him for the night?" Despite protocol in the club, James asked that Sophie never called him a Master. As Grayson owned the majority of it, nobody argued with him.

"Tell your Master that Miss Anderson and I'll escort James home. We'll dress and be out in a minute."

Sonia rose her head and looked towards Sophie. As she was slightly in front of him, Matthew couldn't see the look on Sonia's face, but he saw the wink and smile from Sophie.

"Return to your Master Sophie, or I'll have him enact a rather unfulfilling punishment on you."

She rolled her eyes.

"I was just checking on my girl. You're a big man Matthew."

Sonia laughed and laid back down on his chest.

"Your girl is fine. Now go."

She shut the door. Thankfully the rooms were well sound proofed, or he would be sure he would have heard her telling everyone that they'd finally done it. There were never any sexual secrets between them all. He liked that, though. Lord knows he kept enough other secrets. It was nice just to be honest for once.

"I don't know if I have the energy to get dressed." Sonia hummed into his peck while tracing an imaginary circle around the other. "I wish we could just stay here."

He got out of the bed and looked around for his clothes.

"I'll help you dress in a minute and undress again when we get home. You just rest. You're off duty."

"I can dress myself." She moved the covers back and laid the iced towel down on the bed.

"Listen to your Master, little Miss Stubborn."

She bit her lip.

"Maybe I should let you dress me. It seems my legs have gone to jelly."

"Told you." He retrieved a bottle of water from the fridge and handed it to her. "Drink this."

"Thank you." She took the water, and he put his shirt back on. Sonia watched him the entire time. He picked up her clothes and went over to her.

"Arms up."

He pulled her top over her head. He leant forward and kissed each of her breasts before lowering the silky fabric. Her legs dangled over the edge of the bed, so it was easy to pull her trousers on. He supported her while she stood again and secured them at her waist. She started to shiver. She'd wear no jacket till they got outside, so he pulled the blanket from the end of the bed and wrapped it around her shoulders. "Keep that over you till I can get your coat."

"Thank you, Master."

"No more Master now. Just Matthew."

"Thank you, Matthew."

A little tear tumbled down her cheek.

"What's wrong?"

"Nothing. I'm happy. I feel..." She hesitated on the final word. He searched her, waiting for the answer. "I feel normal."

He brought her chin up and laid a tender kiss on her lips.

"I love you," she whispered. The words were there. They were on the edge of his lips. He opened his mouth to speak. To say them. "I know there is still more to learn and you'll tell me when you're ready. I know until then that you can't reply to what I just said, but the look in your eyes just then told me everything I need to know." She kissed him this time, and he let out the breath he didn't realise he'd been holding.

"We'd better go, before Sophie is sent back in to see if we have gone to sleep. I don't want to be responsible for my cheeky friend being denied an orgasm. Not now I know how good they can be."

"Move into my apartment with me? I don't want to spend any time away from you if I can help it." The words flowed from his lips before he even realised.

"Let's get home and get some sleep. We can talk about

that in the morning when we're not in a blissful post sexual haze."

He nodded, then scooped her up into his arms.

"As long as you stay with me tonight."

CHAPTER FIFTEEN

Sonia

Sonia rolled over in the bed. The ache between her thighs reminded her of what had happened last night.

"Do you need more ice?"

Matthew pulled her into his arms and kissed the top of her head.

"I think I'll be okay."

"I didn't do my job properly then. I'll do better tonight." He chuckled, and she patted lovingly at his chest. See looked over at the clock.

"We better get up. James will want to go to the office soon."

"He knows you stayed the night. Don't worry he'll work from home till I'm ready to take him." He still hadn't opened his eyes.

"What? You're supposed to be at James' beck and call."

"You're worried. Tell me."

My position here is rather precarious. Miranda doesn't really need me and with Amy gone..."

"And coming back soon if I have my way."

"Let me finish."

"James doesn't need me, and I like this job. The family." She lowered her voice, "You being around daily. I don't want to lose it by doing something mundane like staying in bed with you if James doesn't like it. That's why I need time to consider you asking me to move in here."

"You're anxious about this aren't you?"

"I feel settled for the first time in my life. I'm so scared of losing that. I'm torn, Matthew. I want to wake up every morning with your arms wrapped around me. But I'm so afraid of losing what I have."

He let out a long sigh and threw back the sheets. Getting out of the bed, he pulled on a pair of jogging bottoms which were over the back of a chair in the corner of the room. Next, he went to his wardrobe and pulled out a t-shirt and shorts.

"Put these on." He handed her the clothes. The t-shirt would be a dress on her; the shorts were probably not needed.

"Why?" She took the clothes and started to dress.

"Breakfast."

"How is that going to solve my worries?"

"You'll see."

"You keep saying that."

"That is why I'm the Dom, and you're my very willing submissive."

She huffed.

"Who knows as many fancy moves as you to lay you flat out on the floor."

"Try it." He held his arms up welcoming her to attack him.

Matthew followed her out of the bedroom and led her into the kitchen. James was sitting at the breakfast table, studying The Times intently while sipping his coffee. Matthew escorted her to the table.

"Wait there." He left her alone and disappeared into the lounge.

James looked up. She was suddenly very nervous at being dressed in only Matthew's t-shirt and oversized boxer shorts in the middle of her boss' kitchen. James smiled at her, and she embarrassingly returned the greeting. Matthew returned with a cushion, pulled an antique wooden chair out from the table and put the pillow down on it. "Sit."

"If she's sitting on a cushion I don't need to ask if you two had a good evening."

Matthew took a seat next to her and growled at James in response.

"James Thomas North, you leave them alone." Sonia

jumped a little when Miranda suddenly appeared from inside the walk-in larder. "Good morning Matthew, Sonia. What can I get you?"

"Coffee, please," Matthew grunted then looked over to her.

"Um. I."

"She'll have a coffee as well, Mrs North, a splash of milk, no sugar." Matthew reached out under the table and took hold of her leg. She almost jumped out of her skin. "It's okay." His tone was soft and calming; though his eyes conveyed so much more. Her heart stopped beating like it was a freight train on a collision course and returned to a more natural speed.

"A coffee would be good. Is there anything I can help you with Mrs North?"

"Not at all. You relax. If I need help, James can get up. You're a guest here."

Matthew cleared his throat, James furrowed his brows and looked between them.

"Actually, that's something I wanted to talk to you about."

"You didn't win." Grayson's deep masculine voice complained while he led his fiancée into the kitchen.

"I did, too."

"Morning everyone." Sophie breezed over to a seat and Grayson pulled it out for her. Sonia watched as the youngest North sibling smiled up at her fiancé. He took a bowl from her place setting and piled it with fruit from the exotic salad in the centre of the table. He was careful to make sure he took no blueberries. Sonia remembered that Miss North didn't like them. Grayson placed the bowl down in front of Sophie and then handed her a croissant.

"Make sure you eat it all. We had a good workout last night."

"Please, I don't need to hear that when I'm eating my toast." James took a bite and made fake gagging noises.

"He meant at the gym big brother. We went before the

club."

Grayson and Miranda took their seats, and everyone started to help themselves to food from the table. Sonia had never seen such a spread, fruit, croissants, pancakes, cereals, toast with various homemade jams, yoghurts, there were even sausages, bacon and eggs. She sat there feeling a little awkward. Should she just help herself? Grayson had given Sophie her food. This wasn't her home. Matthew leant forward and handed her some toast. He smiled and told her if she wanted anything else to help herself.

"Matthew, you had something you wanted to say?" James spiked at a sausage while his gaze remained firmly fixed on her.

"I hope it's that he's going to take poor Sonia shopping later to get her some decent clothes for when she stays. I remember the first time I stayed at Grayson's; he offered me his dirty pants to put on. They better be clean clothes she's wearing, Matthew Carter."

She wished the ground would open up and swallow her at everyone's comments. She'd spent most of her life just having a bowl of cereal alone in her flat, to have everyone chatting and knowing that she spent last night in Matthew's bed was just utterly embarrassing.

"Sophie, quiet." Grayson silenced his fiancé with one word. "Let Matthew speak."

Matthew moved his hand from her thigh and took her shaking hand in his. "Boss, I was wondering if it would be okay if Sonia moved into my rooms with me?"

"We'll all help her pack and move her belongings in today. It's about time." He popped the sausage into his mouth while continuing to grin.

Miranda came around to Sonia's side of the table and cuddled her.

"It is about time. I'm so happy for you both. You're a proper part of the family now."

Sonia could feel tears starting to form in her eyes. She snuffled.

"Oh no, no tears. This is happy news. Well, it will be, when you get out of those clothes and into something a bit more stylish!" Sophie laughed, then clapped her hands together in excitement. "I know! We can go back to the club tonight and celebrate. Master?" Sonia's eyes widened in fear of what was going to come out of the excitable Miss North's mouth. "Could Sonia and I scene together with you and Master Matthew? It's been so long since we've done a scene with anyone."

"I don't think in front of your mother and brother is the place to discuss that." Grayson rose an eyebrow.

That was all Sonia could take.

"I'm sorry. I need the bathroom." She jumped up from the table and fled back to Matthew's room. He appeared at the door a few seconds after she'd thrown herself on the bed trying to catch her breath.

"Breathe in for four and out for four. Slowly. Focus on your breath." He sat down on the bed next to her.

"Did that just happened?" she spoke through gulps of air.

"Normal breakfast in the North household I'm afraid."

"They're so open. With everything."

"Yes. For a family that hid behind so many secrets for years, they're pretty casual. What do you say?"

"To what?" She finally had her breath under control. Well, as controlled as it was going to be with Matthew moving his hand up and down her leg in reassurance.

"To all of it. Moving in. The club bit if you fancy it."

What did she say to all of that?

She then looked over to Matthew, who sat calmly on the bed, his eyes focused intently on her. "Yes to it all."

CHAPTER SIXTEEN

Matthew

"How about this one?" Sophie held up a tight, and incredibly short, leather dress. Sonia shook her head furiously, so the young Miss North threw the garment onto the ever-growing pile of discarded clothes. Grayson, standing in the corner and supported by the door frame, groaned and went back to texting on his phone. Matthew had been sitting in the same comfortable armchair for an hour now. He, Sophie, and Grayson were dressed and ready to go, but Sonia was still in a dressing gown.

"Grayson, Sophie, can you give us a minute please? What's wrong with the dresses?"

"Nothing."

"You know what happens when you lie."

"I didn't. I didn't lie."

"Sonia."

"I didn't lie, I promise you. There is nothing wrong with the dresses. They're perfect for Sophie but there just not me."

"Wait here." He strode out of the room and called for James. His boss appeared from his study where he was working late after spending the day helping with the move. James had decided that last night had been enough at the club.

"What's wrong?"

"I need a favour. It's a big one. Please say no if you don't feel up to it."

"I don't want to go to the club."

"No, it isn't that." Matthew ran his hand nervously through his hair.

"What is it?"

"The clothes you had me buy Amy--I remember a bright red corset and matching leather leggings."

James swallowed.

"I'm sorry. Forget it. I'll sort something else." He turned to go back to where Sonia was.

"Matthew. Take them."

"I can't."

"Red isn't Amy's colour, anyway. I don't know why I suggested it. Red suits Sonia much better."

"Amy will return. You two-- you're meant for each other. I'll go check on her, talk to her. Or I could send Sonia."

"No. I know you know where she is, but I don't want to know. When she's ready. When we're both ready. It will happen." Matthew thought he could see tears forming in his boss's eyes. "Anyway. Enough of the girly stuff. Go get the clothes and dress up your woman. Have a great night and try not to think of me slaving away at work."

"Yeah, don't worry. I won't think of you at all." He fired back.

After collecting the clothes, he took them back to Sonia. "Are these better?"

"I love you. They're perfect. They're me. I know I'll get naked in the club, and I can handle that, but when I'm just there, I need to hide my scars. They are a part of me and what makes me beautiful. I know that so I don't need a flogging to remind me, but I don't know. I just feel more comfortable in trousers than dresses or skirts."

"Get dressed. I'll send Sophie back in. Grayson and I need to plan."

"That sounds worrying." She picked up the leather leggings and put one foot in the hole.

"No, that sounds promising." He turned to leave.

"Matthew?"

"Yes?"

"I'm going to like living with you. Having someone."

He smiled, he was going to like it also. It had been a long time since he had someone like that. Ever since...no, not tonight. This was Sonia's time. He wouldn't make the same mistakes again.

*

"Master?" Sophie asked Grayson, "are Sonia and I both bottoms tonight or is one of us topping?" They had just finished a discussion on safe words and had installed the traffic light system.

Grayson shrugged his shoulders, "Matthew, what do you think?"

He didn't know. Sonia definitely had the makings of a switch, but the fact that her hand was trembling in his worried him that she wouldn't cope with Sophie's mischievous nature. She tugged on his hand.

"Master."

"You may speak." They'd been sitting in the bar area of the club for around an hour now just watching the scenes going on around them. A Dom was whipping his Sub over a bondage bench. Another was strapping her rather excited Sub into a cock and ball strap. He shuddered. It would be a cold day in hell before anyone did that to his balls. Well, actually when he was training he allowed it to happen, but nobody dared look him in the face or say one word to him while it was attached. Sonia's voice drew him out of his disturbing reflection.

"If I top Sophie that means I can be her Mistress doesn't it?"

"It does."

She looked thoughtful.

"Does Sophie like to be topped by women?"

"You may ask her."

"Sophie, do you like to be topped by women?"

Sophie looked up at Grayson from her kneeling position at his feet. "May I answer her please?"

Grayson let out a belting laugh. "That tells you the answer there, Sonia." Matthew shook his head; he knew that his friend's fiancée was behaving for a particular reason. "You may answer her."

"I would like it very much if you top me."

"I don't believe that was the question you were asked, but you're trying so hard to be good that I'll let it go." Sophie turned to look at Sonia again.

"In answer to your question. I would like to be topped by a woman very much."

"Shall we take this discussion somewhere a little bit more private?" Matthew put his arm protectively around Sonia's shoulders.

"Yes, please Master may we." Sophie was now almost bouncing on her knees.

Grayson led the way through the throng of spectators watching the scenes.

"We'll go to my private room. I think Sonia was on display enough for your liking last night."

She certainly had been. He was glad this was going to be done in seclusion. It was still a steep learning curve for his young Sub, and he didn't want to scare her off.

Grayson opened the door to his room. He had tended to work with James in clubs, although he had witnessed several of Grayson and Sophie's scenes before. Grayson was a true Master of his art. The room was tastefully decorated in natural fibres with a definitely Native American vibe. Despite his past; Grayson was very close to his native roots. He was born into the Navajo tribe and for many years was known as Gini or Hawk as it was translated. Matthew didn't know the full reasons behind why he left and became the famous actor he did, but even though Grayson never spoke of it, he always adhered to his ancestral beliefs.

"Sophie, undress Sonia please," Grayson spoke, but Matthew nodded his approval. They had had a brief discussion earlier on how the evening would go. It wasn't going to be about the men. It was going to be about worshipping the two perfect women they had. The girls had agreed with much enthusiasm.

"Yes, Master."

Grayson and Matthew took seats on leather chairs in the

corner.

Sophie helped Sonia off with her corset. He was surprised to find her not self-conscious but proudly standing before them. Her trousers and thong were removed next, and she stood naked, her head held up high. Sophie folded the clothes up and placed them on the side. She returned to Sonia.

"Go back to your Master please so we can wait for his next instructions."

"Yes, Mistress."

He couldn't help but absorbdy at the bright smile that washed over Sonia's face.

Matthew beckoned Sonia to him with a finger.

"On your knees before Grayson, but I want your back to him."

She obeyed.

"Sophie," Grayson spoke. "I want you to remove your clothes and kneel in front of Sonia."

"Yes, Master."

Matthew shifted his chair so that the two kneeling women were sandwiched between their seats. He could see Sonia's face and Grayson could see Sophie's.

"How sensitive are Sonia's breasts?" Grayson questioned him.

"What are you thinking?"

"Nipple clamps? Sophie looks so beautiful in them."

"Sonia." Grayson allowed him to take over.

"Yes, Master."

"If you would like to wear nipple clamps then you're to ask Sophie to put them on you. I want you to put them on Sophie though. If you're not sure what to do, then you're to ask Master Grayson. Do you understand?" He sat back in the chair, his feet placed firmly on the floor but his legs parted. He took a long sip of his warm brandy. Grayson handed the clamps to Sophie.

"Yes, Master. Sophie, I wish you to put the clamps on me, please. If you do me first, then I'll assist you. Make us pretty for our Masters."

"Yes, Mistress. I like to be decorated for Master Grayson."

"Less chatter, more clamping."

Sophie lowered her head to Sonia's breast and circled her small tongue around the stiffening peak.

"Sweet like sugar. You smell of lavender."

"My favourite perfume."

Sophie ran the nipple through her fingers and placed the clamp over it. Sonia let out a moan. The second clamp was applied; the glazed look already washed over her face. He bet she was already dripping for him.

"Is she wet, Sophie?"

"Touch me and show my Master how much I weep for him already." His cock rammed into the zip of his leather trousers. His little lady had turned into a sex kitten.

"She is sodden. So ready for your cock already." Sophie brought her fingers up to show him where they glistened with arousal.

"Give your fingers to Master Matthew. Allow him to taste his submissive's desire for him." Grayson shifted forward in his seat, his massive forearms resting on his muscular thighs. Sophie brought her fingers to his mouth, and he twisted his tongue around Sonia's honeyed taste. Damn it was the best ever. His cock throbbed. He adjusted, and Grayson curled his lip in a playful smirk at the suffering Matthew was so obviously experiencing.

"My girl tastes so sweet. I think I need more."

Sophie pulled her fingers out of his mouth and went back to Sonia.

"Not yet. Wait."

"Sonia turn around and get on all fours. I want to see my pussy. Sophie's clamps will have to wait."

"She'll be rewarded for her patience. She likes to give more than receive anyway." Grayson brought his lips down onto Sophie's in a promise of what she would get later.

Sonia adjusted her position to that which Matthew had

asked her to. Her most intimate parts were displayed for everyone in the room to see.

"Ask Master Matthew if you may taste his girl? On your knees, crawl to him. I want to watch your pussy while you do." Grayson gently threw her down.

Sophie crawled to Matthew, but he could barely pay attention to her when Sonia was on all fours.

"May I use my mouth on Sonia, Master."

"Yes." Her eyes darkened.

"Thank you."

His breathing became more rapid watching Sophie lick at Sonia's clit.

"She tastes so sweet. Best woman I've ever licked."

Sonia writhed under the touch. Small little groans floating from her lips, every one signalling how much she was enjoying what was happening to her.

"Anal?" Grayson asked. Sonia tightened, her eyes widened.

"I'm prepping, but we're taking things slowly."

"Plugs?"

"Yes."

"What size?"

"Slim."

"Sophie, get me some lube and the slim plug."

"Sophie. Grayson and I get hot when two women kiss. I want you to keep Sonia's mouth entertained. Sonia, I'm going to fuck you. Grayson is going to put the plug in your arse and play with it. We want you to feel full."

"I want all of that please, Master. Especially your cock."

"May I play with her breasts and the clamps as well Masters?"

"Good idea, Sophie. I'm in agreement if Grayson is."

"Yes." Grayson was busy rubbing the lube around the plug. "Do you want to put it in?"

"No, I'll go suit up."

"Condom?"

"We need to have the doctor's appointment."

"Go there tomorrow man. That pussy needs fucking bareback."

He pulled down his trousers and glided his hand up and down his rigid length a few times before placing the condom on. He was listening the whole time to Sonia, moaning as her puckered hole swallowed up the plug.

"Ready?" Grayson asked.

He nodded and placed himself at her entrance. In one long, slow thrust he pushed inside. He could feel the plug against his cock.

Sophie leant forward and tugged on one of Sonia's clamped nipples. Their mouths crashed at the same time, feminine delicacy abandoned to a burning desire. Boy, was that hot. He started to thrust. Grayson took the end of the plug, and as Matthew pushed his cock into her pussy, Grayson pulled the plug almost out of her anus. The three of them worked together, driving Sonia towards a rapid and explosive climax. Just as she came down, they sent her over again. She was thrashing, screaming so loudly that despite the soundproofed walls he was sure people would hear. On the third orgasm, he followed her over.

CHAPTER SEVENTEEN

Sonia

"Sonia, are you ready to go?" Matthew called out. She was busy searching through her chest of drawers.

"Five minutes. I just need to get Miranda's leaflets for her coffee morning." Where the hell were they? She'd been living with Matthew for a month now and had gotten far too comfortable already. There was nothing for it. She would have to empty the entire drawer. Pulling it out, she turned it over and let the bits of paper, hairbands, random coins, odd cables, and a selection of keys and sweets tumble onto the floor. Frantically she searched through the mess. "Where is it?"

"Sonia. What are you doing?" Matthew appeared at the door. He sighed and frowned at the chaos she had created.

"What!" She exclaimed. "Everyone has that one drawer you put everything in for safekeeping. You have a whole cupboard." She waved her hands in the air towards the direction of his wardrobe.

"You can't find what you're looking for because I gave the leaflets to Miranda earlier. You put them out on the bed this morning."

"What?" The words spat out disbelievingly. "I don't remember that."

"Probably because you did it just after I'd had my tongue in that beautiful little pussy of yours."

She snarled at him. "You could have told me you were taking them. I've just spent the last ten minutes searching."

"What's this? Her Majesties Prisons?" The flushing receded at a dramatic pace to be replaced by a chill so cold she felt like she would freeze. He held up a piece of paper she knew only too well what it contained. "Sonia?"

"It's nothing." Everything was back in the drawer. She wanted to snatch the paper back from Matthew but knew better than to do that. She stood and started to put the drawer back.

"Drop the drawer now. Turn around and get on your knees. You're lying." Damn, Dom sixth sense. She was risking it, but she ignored him. This was foolish and she'd never done it before but now wasn't the time. They both had jobs to do. Shoving the drawer roughly back into place, she grabbed her bag and stormed from the room. Matthew stalked behind her down the corridor. She could feel the heat radiating off him. His nostrils were probably flaring that he had been ignored. She was so going to end up with a bright red arse and not in a good way. She couldn't talk about this, though. It was her past.

"Come on Miranda. Let's go. I don't want you to be late for your meeting." She smiled cheerfully.

Mrs North senior went pale and swallowed. Miranda looked behind Sonia and took a step backwards.

"James, I think you better take me."

"Matthew?" James enquired.

"She's lied and isn't telling me something."

"I'll take mum and stay with her till you show up. Take as long as you need."

"Will do. I'll text you when we leave."

James and his mother left her and Matthew alone. Silence. Nothing except Sonia's heart trying to beat out of its chest and the aura surrounding Matthew threatening to explode. He prowled around her so that he stood in front of her, not behind her. She quickly looked down to the floor. He grabbed her chin and tilted it up so that she had no choice but to look at him.

"What is this?" He waved the paper at her.

This was nothing to do with him.

"I asked you a question."

"You have eyes, read it for yourself."

"Don't make your punishment worse. You're already at

twenty for walking away from me."

"You can't spank me for this."

"Who's talking about spanking? I'm talking the whip."

She inhaled sharply.

"Last chance. What is this?"

Punishment with the whip meant that he wouldn't allow her to drift into subspace. He would make her count. She didn't like it when he did that.

"It's a visiting order."

"This was for last week. Did you go?"

"No," She looked back down to the floor.

"Lift your head and look at me." She was defeated and in the space where her brain had no choice but to tell her body to obey his commanding tone. Her head wouldn't move to look away but she managed to shut her eyes.

"Open them." The darkness in his voice gave no leeway. The frustration she was feeling bubbled over. Her voice raised, and she spun round, storming back to the bedroom. "This is none of your business. I don't want to visit him even if he sends me a hundred orders." She paused at the entrance to their bedroom. Her bag fell off her shoulder and slipped to the floor.

Her legs started to burn, the cuts calling her to open them. Matthew brought his muscular arms tightly around her. Sheltering her from the pain she was feeling. She struggled against him. Needing to get away. Needing pain, not comfort.

"I'm here." He whispered into her ear. "I'm here."

"He killed her."

"I know."

"I saw it all. The glass the way it cut her. The screams of agony mixing with his angry yells. His eyes, they were dead the entire time. Glossed over with the drink. He didn't even realise what he was doing."

"It's okay. I'm here."

"I can't visit him. I can't. How can he be my father? I can't even go back to the house but I can't bring myself to sell it."

"Sorry?" His voice was confused.

"The house was signed over to me when I turned eighteen. He said he wanted me to have money should I need it. I was going to go there and clean it out before selling it but I couldn't. As far as I know nobody has been there since the day my mother died."

"Twenty years ago."

"Yes."

"You're running away from your past. Trying to bury what happened in the sand. You'll never get over it until you face it. Sonia you need to see your father and go back to the house."

She knew that she shouldn't feel this way but that comment angered her.

"I'm running away from my past." She pulled out of his arms. It was a bit of a struggle as he was reluctant to let her go but he seemed to sense the change in her mood. "Can you get any more hypocritical. At least I faced up to what happened in my past. You can't even admit you love me to my face because you hide behind yours. You want to talk about burying the past then look no further than yourself." She stomped over the bed. She wasn't going to let him touch her. The bastard, one rule for her and another for him.

"There's a difference."

"How." She screamed at him.

He came forward and knelt at her feet. "I admit I hide behind my past. I know I can't say I love you yet because of it. But I don't want to bury my head in the sand any longer. Sonia, allow me to help you with this and then together we will work through what happened to me."

"Let's sort you first?"

"You know how stubborn I am. It has to be you first. I have to know that you'll be able to handle everything that I throw at you when I tell you what happened."

"That's just your male ego speaking. Fix the women

first."

"I wish it were the case. But it isn't."

"I don't think I can see my father."

"You don't have to make that decision yet. How about we go to the house first. See how you feel when you're there and see it again."

"I should sell it. Mum would hate her precious kitchen not being used for cooking. It's probably a wreck by now. I'll have to get someone in to decorate and check it all out structurally. It has been severely neglected for twenty years."

"I think we might know someone that can help us with that."

"Hand it over to James? Great idea. He can go and sort everything out instead of me."

"No, you need to go. You need to find closure."

"Damn you." She slid off the end of the bed and into his lap. "When do you want to go?"

"I'll arrange with James for us to go tomorrow."

"So soon."

"We have a lot to face. We need to do it before we change our minds."

"Ok, but no more talk of my father. I'm not ready to face him."

"Okay."

"We should get to James and Miranda."

"Not yet."

"Matthew."

"You lied, that requires punishment."

"Seriously?"

"Yes. Beside. I think Miranda will absolutely love showing James off to all the lady friends. I can just picture all the cheek pinching He'll get. It will do him good."

Sonia couldn't keep in a little chuckle at that thought.

"I'm sorry for not telling you about the visiting order. I've always just ignored them and put them in a drawer till I threw them away."

"We've both lived separate existences, insular in our needs for far too long. It's going to take getting used to. We will fight. I will stomp and shout. You'll throw tantrums and slam drawers, but ultimately we will come back to this." He wrapped his arms around her and pulled her in for a kiss. "Now remove your clothes. I think I made it a count of thirty for disobedience."

"Really." She pushed back from him, her bottom smarting at the thought but her core clenched with the knowledge of the pleasure it will bring. Matthew's voice turned dark.

"Now Sonia."

This time she obeyed.

CHAPTER EIGHTEEN

Matthew

"I think I'm going to be sick." Matthew slammed on the brakes of the Harley-Davidson Lowrider. Sonia jumped off and whipped her helmet over her head. She flung it on the floor and bent over, the vile vomit projecting from her mouth onto the floor. He secured the bike, took a bottle of water along with some tissues from in the storage compartment and helped settled his poorly girlfriend. She was white as a sheet.

"I'm sorry." He could see that she was fighting back the tears.

"You've nothing to be sorry about."

"I'm so nervous."

"It's a big step you're taking. I'll be with you the entire time, though."

"I don't think I can do it."

"Do I need to give you a reminder of how strong you are?"

"No."

"Drink this." He passed her the water and wiped her forehead.

"Let's go." Before he could help Sonia to her feet, a Land Rover pulled up next to the bike. A tiny lady jumped out. Her mouth dropped, eyes wide she stumbled over to them.

"Aye, it be a ghost." The woman started to drop down to the ground, but he jumped up and caught her. "Sonia?"

"Yes."

"Thee be the spitting image of tha ma. God rest 'er soul."

"I know you?"

"Yer did. Mary Scott, I live on the farm next to yours. Thee going tha?"

Sonia nodded.

"I knew tha'd come back one day. Me husband and I've been looking after it. Tha Ma would have hated to see it fall into disrepair. I can't believe how much yer look like 'er."

Sonia looked down. Matthew helped Mrs Scott to stand.

"I'm sorry. I don't know yer."

"I'm Matthew Carter, Sonia's partner."

"Pleasure to meet tha, Mr Carter."

"Matthew, please Mrs Scott."

"Then tha call me Mary."

"I will do."

"I'm just going to clean up a bit more. I won't be a minute. You head back to the car and bike. I'll follow."

"She okay, love?" Mary lowered her voice and leant into him to whisper her question as they returned to the vehicles.

"Nervous."

"Tha knows everything."

"I do."

"Poor child. I remember when they brought 'er out. So much blood. She just thought 'er Ma was sleeping."

"You've been looking after the house?"

"Her father sent me a letter from prison. He's such a wazzock. I 'ad a key to the house already. Told me 'e would sign it over to Sonia as soon as 'e could. Asked if we could look after it. Sell what we needed to cover the costs. We ran it as the farm it was. My son was sixteen. He's taken on most of the running of the place. We wondered about 'im moving in there, but it didn't feel right. I tried to find where she was but I just couldn't. Is she 'ere to sell it?"

"I don't know yet."

"I'll go ahead and unlock for thee. Then get out of the way. Come over to our place afterwards, love. "I'll give thee tha tea an' tha's welcome t'stay"

"Thank you. I really appreciate that. But we can easily find a B&B. I don't want to trouble you."

"I'll get a bed med up for thee. It's no trouble."

"Thank you." Mary drove away. Sonia reappeared.

"I don't really have any photos of my mum. I have my memories of her, but I never thought I looked like her. I hope there are some at the house."

"I'm sure there will be. It sounds as though Mrs Scott and her family have really looked after the place."

"I'm glad of that."

"You ready to go?"

"As I'll ever be."

It didn't take them long to reach the house.

"It seems so much smaller than I remember."

"You were only five when you were last here. Everything always seems smaller as an adult than to a child. You ready to go in?"

"If I said no would we get back on the bike and go home?"

He gave her a look which told her the answer to that question.

"I didn't think so."

Matthew opened the door for her. The décor on the walls could do with a bit of a re-vamp, but the place was clean. He'd not been expecting that. Sonia stepped over the threshold and let out a long breath.

"Where do you want to do?" He cooed, not wanting to scare her or make her run.

"I need to go straight in don't I. Face the demons?"

He nodded.

"This way." She led him down the corridor towards a closed door and opened it. He watched her carefully as her eyes fell to a particular spot on the floor. She let out a deep breath before chewing on the edge of her lip.

"I thought there would still be blood."

"I believe Mrs Scott has cleared it all up." The room looked spotless. He suspected that the generous lady came and cleaned at least once a week.

"I sat here for ages. I thought she was sleeping. She looked so peaceful. Why did this happen?"

"It isn't an excuse, but your father had an illness. It wasn't understood then as it is now."

"She was barely older than I am now. It wasn't fair. I can't even accurately remember her." A tear left Sonia's eye and tumbled down her cheek. She wiped it away. This time he brought her into his arms. He didn't speak. She needed to do that. "I can smell her in here. She always wore jasmine perfume. It was funny because at the end of the day it was mixed with the smell of baking. That was my mum's smell." She turned to nestle further into his arms. "I remember the day before she died, well I think I do. I don't know if it is true or not. Dad was out on the farm. He was having a good day. We'd had a massive Sunday roast together, and he'd gone out to tend the animals. Mum and I made fresh soup from vegetables from the garden, onions, carrots, leeks, a bit of garlic, stock and herbs. I was five, soup seemed like the devil's food to me then, but I still helped. We made fresh bread to go with it. I remember her showing me how to knead the dough. We both ended up throwing it around the table." She paused and sniffed. He ran a hand down her hair. "I remember we sat down that evening as a family. We laughed. Dad even read me a story. I guess it was the calm before the storm. I'm glad I have that memory, though. Shows I did have a normal family sometimes. Why does it hurt so much, Matthew?"

"I wish I could take your pain away from you. Make it easier at least. Only you can do that, and that's why it hurts so much. You love both your mother and father."

"I don't love my dad."

"Did you not love him when he ate the bread and soup you helped make. When he read you the story?"

"I haven't loved him since he killed my mother. He doesn't deserve it anymore."

"Sonia."

"I'll never forgive him. Please don't ask me to." She stood, shoulders slumped by the door. "I'll never get the image of her laying on the floor out of my head. It haunts

my dreams. I have no father. "She pushed him away and got up. "I'm going to get a few bits, and I want to see my room."
He sighed as she left the kitchen. She was stubborn but understandably so. He just knew from experience until you forgave you couldn't move on.

"Matthew?"

Sonia called out, she was distressed. He quickly got up and ran to where the sound of her voice was coming from.

"It hasn't changed."

"What hasn't?"

"My room." He peered in the door that she held open.
"My toys are still here. My bedcovers." She opened a wardrobe. "My clothes. It's like time stood still."

"I never figured you as being a pink girl." It was a very girly room. "I thought you'd have action men."

She laughed at this one before breaking down in floods of tears. He just held her. He didn't know for how long, but it was what she needed. His warmth, his love, his reassurance.

"John, get yer feckless arse in 'ere. Supper's up." Mary called out as Matthew and Sonia took their seats at the table a few hours later.

"I'm coming." Mary's husband replied and ambled into the kitchen. "Parkin, me favourite. Good lass."

"Don't yer good lass me. Sit down so I can serve yer. Where's Jack?"

"On 'is way. Was just finishing up the feeding."

"Well, 'e better hurry or tha be nout left with yer appetite."

"Ere." Mary slapped her husband's hand when he reached out for the cake." Guests first. Matthew, Sonia?"

"Thank you, Mary." He took a piece of the gingerbread tea loaf for himself and served Sonia. After the afternoon she was weak and drained. He just wanted to get some food into her and then get her to bed. They'd made the right decision to stay here the night rather than travel back.

"Ma? Dad?"

A deep masculine voice came from the hallway.

"In 'ere?"

Matthew knew that he was big, but the man that entered the room barely fitted through the doorway. He was a ball of pure muscle.

"Well feck me, little seesaw came home." Everyone looked towards him. Sonia who was mid-bite of cake dropped it to her plate.

"Jack, manners." His mum chastised.

"Sorry, ma." He replied and took his seat.

"Little seesaw?" Matthew asked.

"It was what I used to call Sonia."

"I remember," Sonia spoke up. "Jack called me it because whenever I came around here, he had to spend hours playing with Harry and me on the one in their back garden."

"It's still out there yer know. Ma's hoping one of us eventually give her grandbabies."

"You're not married?"

"Disgrace ain't it. Thirty-six and still living at home."

Matthew wrapped an arm around Sonia's shoulder. He'd never felt jealousy before, but these two remembered each other and Jack was a big man. He wasn't a part of this conversation.

"I almost forget. Jack, this is my partner Matthew. Matthew this is Jack. He's the one that has been looking after the farm."

Jack wiped his hands on his trousers and reached over the table to shake Matthews. He returned the greeting

"Pleasure to meet yer."

"Your accent isn't as broad as your parents."

"I took a year out in London with my brother Charlie, he lived down that way. Lost a bit of the tongue then. Lots of southerners up 'ere now that I deal with so easier for 'em to understand."

"Yes, we are a simple bunch that prefer our language just as we are used to it."

"I 'ad a great laugh watching Charlie trying to chat this

lass up once in a club in London. She didn't have a clue what he was saying. Needless to say 'e didn't get owt that night."

"Poor Charlie. Is he still in London?"

"He moved back last year. Works in York."

"What about Harry, George, Sam and Ellie?"

"How many siblings do you have?" Matthew spluttered into his coffee.

"There be five of 'em." John smacked his lips together as he spoke, "My lass did 'er duty."

"More like you couldn't keep yer 'ands off me."

"Ma. We don't need to know that." Jack put his head in his hands. "They're all still around the area. We went separate ways for a while but all came back."

"The place has that pull. Even if you want to get away, you can't." Sonia put her head down, her eyes watered again.

"I'm sorry about what happened. If I could've done anything to 'elp."

"You have done so much. Your mum said you've been looking after the farm."

"I 'ave. It's a good little earning. Yer Dad asked us to set up an account to pay the profits into after I took a wage and costs."

"And then he used the rest trying to buy alcohol in prison."

"No, lass." Mary interrupted. "Yer dad stopped drinking shortly after 'e went to prison. E's been writing to me. I'm not saying 'e didn't slip at first, but e's been dry for ten years now. 'E loved yer ma, 'e 'ates himself for what happened. Yer can't punish 'im more tha 'e is 'imself." Mary pushed her chair back and went to a drawer in an old style dresser. She pulled out a wad of papers. "This be 'is letters. Read 'em, lass. Please. Before yer made any decisions."

CHAPTER NINETEEN

Sonia

"Is it really time to go? I barely feel like I've slept." Sonia rubbed at her tired eyes.

They'd been awake most of the night. Matthew had read the letters to her.

"I'm glad I read them. I can see that he is truly sorry. The first few letters he still blamed my mother but the ones when he stopped drinking showed his real remorse. He misses her, he'll never forgive himself for what he did. I think the next time he sends me a visiting order I'll go and see him. I can't guarantee that I'll go through with it when I get there, but he is my father. I owe him a chance to explain." She looked down at the floor, moments of thought drifting through her head at the words that she had read. He'd spoken of their courtship and how much they'd fallen in love. The drink wasn't an issue at first, but it became so when he started to drink far too much, and the farm began to suffer.

"That's a brave decision." Matthew reached out his hand to assist her onto the bike. "You don't have to wait, though."

He hadn't got on the bike yet but stood in front of her. She narrowed her eyes at him.

"What do you mean?" She stepped off the bike again.

"Are you certain you want to see your father?"

"I think I owe it to us both to put closure to this."

Matthew pulled his phone out. He held a finger up to silence her and placed the phone on speaker so that she could hear.

"Jasper."

"Mr Carter, what can I do for you? Or are you going to do something for me?"

"Haven't I done enough?"

"Probably. What is it? I can't talk for long. The head honcho wants us ready for a briefing in five minutes."

"It won't take long. I need a prison visit today."

"Which one?"

Matthew placed a hand over the phone.

"What prison is your father in?"

"Wakefield."

He removed his hand.

"I need to get into Wakefield. My girlfriend wants to see her father."

"Does he want to see her?"

"He's been sending visitor's orders."

"Can't she use one of them?"

"She destroyed them."

"Give me his name."

"Simon Anderson."

"I call you back ASAP."

"What about your meeting?"

"I've got a pressing matter I need to deal with now. His Highness will have to wait."

Matthew chuckled. "He always did act like he was God. I can't imagine what he's like with their real Highnesses."

"I can only imagine. I won't be long."

The line went dead.

"Today. Now." Her heart was suddenly beating rather rapidly and her palms moistened with nerves. "Surely we have to give more notice?"

"Not when your ex-MI5 and your contacts still are." He pulled her close to him, his warmth soothing her fears. "I'll be with you the entire time. I'm proud of you for making this decision."

"It is the right thing to do isn't it?" She lay her head on his solid chest.

"You hold so much guilt inside you, blaming yourself for something that wasn't within your control. An innocent by-stander. No matter how many times you replay it, you couldn't have changed the outcome. Destiny is the darkness that engulfs us." She pulled back from him and looked up into his eyes. They had gone blank; he couldn't see her movement. He was lost in a world of his own pain.

"Matthew." She whispered. "You lost someone."

"Yes." The phone rang, and she could've cursed. He pushed away from her and answered it.

"Matthew Carter."

"You are in. Get there as soon as you can."

"Thank you. I owe you one."

"I actually think we're probably about even."

"Give it a week."

Matthew hung up and got on the bike. "You ready?"

*

The door opened and a guard walked in, behind him stood an elderly man, his face sunken and the shadows around his eyes thick with regrets. Lines marked his battered face, each one telling a story.

"God help me." He exclaimed when he saw her and staggered back against the wall. The guard moved to his side and helped him to his seat. She remained glued to her seat, her eyes transfixed on the man that was once her father. "Of all the punishments, this is by far the greatest. Your mother, you're like her twin. She wouldn't have been much older than you when she died." He paused, "When I killed her."

With those word's Sonia's regard flashed back to her father. Sorrow filled his eyes, guilt and penitence echoing in the dull green irises. A colour that matched her own.

"You admit it?"

"Yes. I alone am responsible for the death of my wife and your mother. Lost the two people that meant the world to me."

I survived." It was all she could answer.

"But I lost you from my life. I missed all the happy moments of seeing you grow up. Your first day at school, your first lost tooth, date, graduation. I don't even know what you do for a living. Is the man you're with your husband? Do you have children of your own? The demons that I thought I lost at the bottom of a bottle robbed me of that."

"And my mother." She was not going to let his self-pity control her emotions.

"I'm sorry. I wallow on my own grief. I deserve none of those first moments because I took them away from you and your mother. What I did was wrong."

"It was. I'll never be able to fully forgive you for it. You know that, don't you."

"I would never ask you to."

A silence descended on them both. This was harder than she had thought it would be. The man in front of her might be her father but he was also a stranger.

"Mr Anderson. I'm Matthew Carter."

Her father smiled at Matthew. It seemed such an effort for him, though physically not in a bad way.

"It is a pleasure to meet you, Mr Carter." He tried to raise his hand to shake Matthew's but the guard, still in the room, barked "No touching'."

"Why did you keep asking me to come and see you?"

"To apologise." He ran a hand over his bald head. "But it seems so insignificant and worthless now that you're here. Apologies will not change what happened."

"Nothing will change what happened."

"Why did you decided to come and see me now?"

"I went to the house yesterday. I saw Mrs Scott; she gave me the letters that you had sent her. " She pursed her lips together. The bitterness built inside her, bubbling in a manner that threatened to explode. He killed her mother. He should die, painfully, preferably. "You killed her." She screamed so loudly the noise startled even her. "I watched the bottle. You kept plunging it into her; she was screaming in agony. She hadn't done anything wrong except love you. I hadn't done anything wrong except love you. You're a monster. You deserve to die. I want you dead. Not her." Tears flooded down her cheeks. She crumbled to the floor.

Matthew was instantly there, his arms surrounding her in a comforting cocoon.

Her father huddled over in his chair and started to cough.

"Oh God," Matthew whispered above her head.

Two other guards had appeared. They had breathing apparatus and were hooking him up to it. That is when she noticed it. The blood, red, a wine of life ebbing out of her father.

"Daddy?" The child's innocent phrase slipped from her lips. "What's happening? What's going on?"

"Miss Anderson, please take a seat. Let us stabilise him."

"Stabilise?"

"Sonia." Matthew took her hand and wrapped his arms around her again.

"Why is he like this? What's going on?"

"Wait a moment."

"You know what's wrong?"

She searched him.

"I have my suspicions."

"Tell me." She pursed her lips angrily together.

"Sonia." He father's voice broke through the gasps for air. "I know you'll never forgive me." He stopped to catch his breath again when it caught in his throat. "God has seen fit to enact his own judgement on me. You wish me dead, it will happen. Soon."

"What?"

"I'm riddled with cancer. I have a few months left at best."

"Cancer. What treatment have they given you?"

"None."

"That can't happen."

"It can and it has."

"No." She turned to Matthew. "Can we speak to James? Get his doctor to look at him."

Matthew shook his head. "This is your father's decision."

"I died the night I took your mother's life. My body has

just taken a long while to catch up with my soul."

"I don't want you to die. I didn't mean what I said." Her voice sounded so small.

"I know. This is what must happen. I'm just glad I got to see the amazing woman you've become. You make sure he looks after you." His eyes flicked to Matthew who was standing against the wall.

"He'll always do that."

"She is safe with me, Mr Anderson."

"I'm tired. I need to sleep. Go live your life. Enjoy every moment of it. The past has shaped you, but don't allow it to destroy you."

"I want to see you again."

"No. We have made our peace with each other. Allow me to die and reconcile with your mother."

The guards returned and helped her father to a wheel chair. They supported all his weight. She tried to keep her composure. To allow him to see her for the last time as the strong woman, he was proud of.

"Sleep well, daddy."

He turned his head, the corners of his mouth turning up into a smile.

Sonia's father died two days later.

The funeral was a very quiet affair. James and Miranda had joined them at the graveside along with the Scott family; he was buried next to her mother. Jack was in the process of buying the farmhouse from her; it was another memory she wanted to put in the past.

CHAPTER TWENTY

Matthew

"Matthew, can you put that box of cupcakes over here please." Miranda's instruction brought him out of his reflection. "James are they the Macaroons. They go over here. Please be gentle with them. They're so delicate, and I don't want to have to discount them."

"Yes, mother."

"Yes, Mrs North."

Both men did as they were told.

"Please say your mother isn't really considering doing this more than once a year?"

"I can't tell a lie to you, my friend, you know that." James started to put the macaroons out on the stand but not before rolling his eyes in annoyance.

"I think we need to seriously discourage her. There must be some sort of security threat I can worry her with. Cakes can easily be used to hold bombs?"

"She makes most of the cakes herself, and she would just have you scan them."

"Any of those attending could injure her?"

"The event is ticketed, and you've examined the guest list in detail?"

"Cakes lead to cholesterol and heart attack?"

"James," Miranda shouted before his boss had a chance to reply. "You don't lay them out like that. In circles, alternate the colours. Make them look attractive to those buying them. I thought that you were supposed to be good at design?" She tutted.

"I'm not. I pay people to do it. Just like we should have done for this."

"I can't pay people!" She looked horrified at the suggestion. "It's for charity. We need to be seen to be doing all we can. Only last week Mrs Morgan held a charity dinner in her home, and she actually waited on the tables herself. What would it look like if I hired people to do it instead of doing it myself?"

"Sensible," James mumbled under his breath and Matthew tried not to smirk. "Mum, we don't need to compete with the likes of Mrs Morgan. I give at least double what her husband gives to charity a year in just a month. We help as many people as we can and in lots of different ways. A little extra help wouldn't be frowned on."

"I'm being totally over the top aren't I?" His mother slumped down onto a chair.

"Just a little, Mrs North." Matthew couldn't stop the answer from coming out of his mouth.

"Mum, you want this event to be a success and it will be but one macaroon out of place will not be a disaster and asking for a little help won't be either."

"I won't be able to get assistance at such short notice. It's going to be a disaster." The matriarch of their little group placed her head in her hands.

"Should ask all the Dom's from the club to help. That would get all the patron's talking, and definitely make it an afternoon tea not to forget." Sonia appeared at the doorway, partially hidden by an enormous croquembouche. I know I wouldn't mind being served cake by a topless hunk." She winked at him, and he made a mental note to collect a few leftovers for later.

"That isn't a bad idea actually." Miranda had lifted up her head, and he could feel her also measuring him up as a topless cake serving waiter.

"Is this what it feels like to a woman when we stare at her boobs?" He queried of James.

"I'm just glad they're all staring at you and not me."

"James, do you think you could arrange it?"

"I'll have to call in a few favours."

"But you could do it. You and Matthew can help out as

well. Such good boys." Sonia placed the croquembouche down, and he watched her laughing thinking she had hidden behind it. He raised an eyebrow at her which told her in no uncertain terms she was being tied up and flogged tonight.

"I'm not wandering around here topless mum, but I will see if I can get some people to help." James pulled out his phone; his mum shoved him out of the way and proceeded to organise the macaroons.

"I'm not going out there like this." Matthew growled.

"Shouldn't it be me telling you that you're not allowed to flash your body to other women?" Sonia ran a hand down his bare chest and stopped at the waistband of his trousers. She pressed a kiss to his left nipple.

"Fuck, now I'm going out there with a hard on."

"Too much information, Matthew." Callum, one of the Doms from the club called out while pumping his pecs.

"And I don't need to watch you flexing those weak, arse excuse for muscles."

"Jealous."

"Yeah right."

"I donna know what ye lads are worried about. I'm wearing a kilt!" Blair interrupted their protestations. "I goona end up flashing me hooded bandit."

"Hooded bandit?" Callum questioned, Matthew, laughed knowing full well what the Scot was referring to.

"You know, me willy."

"Come on boys. Showtime." Miranda stood in the doorway sniggering. They filed out, each taking a tray of cakes as they went. Matthew watched the Mayor of Kensington's wife pinch James' bottom.

"Mr Carter?" A hand tapped him on the leg.

"Mrs Hurlington-Webb. It's good to see you again."

"It's good to see rather a lot of you." He chuckled and handed her a chocolate cake.

"Did I guess right?"

"Of course."

"Miss Anderson is looking somewhat enervated."

"She has had a death in her family recently. It has caused her a lot of stress."

"You must take her on holiday. Replenish her puissance."

"I was thinking the same thing this morning."

"Don't just think it, young man. Just thinking will do that poor girl no good."

"I'll talk to James later about time off."

"I'll phone Miranda tomorrow to ensure that you have." She gave him a small wink and he placed the cakes on the table. A pinch to his bottom, elicited a low growl.

"Mrs Morgan, if you're going to pinch my backside." He hesitated while leaning closer to her. "At least give it a good grab." The ladies all started to laugh again as he turned and presented his backside for closer inspection to the now red-cheeked woman. All the women now came over to have a feel. Out of the corner of his eye, he caught Sonia watching him, a hand resting on her heart. Her lips parted, and she ran her tongue over them. They were going to have a good night. He pulled away from the ladies, and they returned to their gossip and cakes. James was standing over by the drinks table. He had lipstick kisses all over his chest.

"I don't think I want to ask what happened to you."

"I don't want to relive it either."

"Is your mother happy?"

"Ecstatic. They doubled the funds raised last year. We're going to be a regular thing, apparently."

"Damn it."

James handed him a beer.

"I was wondering if Sonia and I could take a week or so off?"

"When?"

"As soon as possible. I'm going to take her to France. Meet my parents. Then, yes. I'm going to tell her everything. It's time."

CHAPTER TWENTY-ONE

Matthew

"What do you fancy next?" Sonia unlocked her phone. They'd been listening to Matthew's choice of music since they'd left Poitiers three hours ago, and it was time for something different.

"I don't mind. You can choose."

"I thought my taste in music was spectacularly wrong?"

"When you play show tunes it is."

"What is wrong with the Wicked soundtrack?"

"Do I even need to answer that?" Matthew smirked but kept his eyes on the road in front of them.

"Just for that, and the fact that we're in France, Les Miserables soundtrack, it is." She giggled as the thunderous beat of 'Look Down' beat out the car stereo.

"You know you'll suffer for this."

"Only after your ear drums have." And she turned the volume up. He used the controls on the wheel to turn it back down. "Spoilsport."

They had borrowed James' Aston Martin for the journey, at their boss' insistence, so she reached over and used her credit card to pay the toll and the barrier rose.

"They should charge on the M25; might lessen the amount of time I have to spend sitting in traffic when Miranda's off on one of her excursions to the gardens with the other ladies."

"It probably won't make much difference actually. We're just too small a country for the number of vehicles on the roads."

"France has definitely been easier to travel in. How long have you been coming here?"

"My parents moved here after they retired but we've

come here since I can remember to see mum's family. I've spent many a summer helping out in the winery."

"Do they still crush the grapes with their feet?"

"No, my family have a machine that does that now. My grand-père's feet weren't exactly hygienic. There is a festival during picking season though where they still do some by feet. I'll have to see if I can bring you to see it."

"I'd like that very much."

The expanse of symmetrically laid vine plantations loomed in front of them as they drove further and further into the countryside leaving behind the alternating fields of vines and asparagus they had been seeing for the last thirty minutes or so.

Matthew turned a corner, and a sea of sunflower heads, illuminated by the vibrant afternoon sun revealed themselves to her. "Oh my God. So many of them. What do they grow them for?"

"Oil mainly."

"Can we stop, please? I want to take a picture."

"Of course." Matthew pulled the car over.

She jumped out of the car and stood beside the field. Matthew turned the engine off and joined her. He wrapped his arms around her waist pulling her against his hard body.

"They are beautiful."

"Tu es belle. Je t'aime." He whispered into her ear and pressed kisses against her cheek.

His hands lowered over her hips, pulling her tightly against him.

"Je pense que ta mère préférerait que tu rentres à la maison d'abord."A masculine voice came from behind them, and she jumped back.

"Putain. Oncle Henri. I'll go see my mother soon."

"I don't think that's any way to speak to your Uncle." The two men drew each other into a warm embrace, kissing each other's cheeks in a traditional French greeting and thumping each other's back in a not so traditional one. "Your aunt Lourdes and your mother have been cooking all your favourite dishes since first thing this morning. It has been such a long time and to be bringing such a belle femme with you." Matthew's uncle reached over and brought her into the traditional greeting now. "As my nephew isn't introducing me himself, allow me. I'm Henri Bresson. My sister is Matthew's mother."

"I'm Sonia Anderson. I'm Matthew's girlfriend. It's lovely to meet you." Henri had come from the direction of the sunflower fields. "Are these your fields?"

"Yes. From the Chateaux to as far as the eye can see."

"Wow. Matthew told me his family had a winery, but I didn't realise you grew other crops. The sunflowers are just stunning."

"Do you want to come back on the tractor with me?"

"She'll be safer in the car," Matthew answered before she could.

"Tres bien. A bientôt."

"See you later, Uncle." Matthew led her back to the car. He opened the door for her, but before she got in, she stood on her tiptoes and kissed him.

"What was that for?"

"For being you."

"Get in the car before I change my mind about going to the house and find the nearest hotel and fuck you till morning."

That took the breath out of her chest.

It didn't take them long to get to the winery. The driveway leading up to it had meandered through a forest before the horizon opened up to expose a large farmhouse surrounded by neatly organised vines.

"This is your family's?"

"Yes. Welcome to the Chateaux Maison Du Bresson. My mother's ancestral home."

A small woman with jet black hair and a dark tan threw herself at Matthew when he got out of the car. "It's so good to see you, mon petit. It's been far too long." Matthew greeted the woman whom Sonia assumed was his mother. A tall gentleman that could only be described as pale looking and British greeted him next.

"Hi, Dad. Mama. Aunt Lourdes. I'd like to introduce my girlfriend, Sonia Anderson."

"Right, inside everyone. We have cheeses and bread ready to be eaten. I'll serve dinner later, but I know that it has been such a long journey for you both so you must be hungry.

"That would be lovely Mrs Carter." Despite stopping on the way down her tummy started to rumble at the thought of a snack.

"Phillip, I hope you opened the vintage 2010 when I told you so that it could breathe. I'm sure they're both in need of a drink as well. "

The bottle was not only opened but had been decanted, and a selection of cheeses were laid out before her.

"When are you two marrying?" Aunt Lourdes hovered over Matthew, filling his plate with more food.

"I think that's a bit premature."

"Zut alors, Matthew. You're not getting any younger. This isn't the first...."

"Aunt." Matthew's abrupt interruption made Sonia jump. "Sonia and I will discuss marriage when are ready to. At the moment, we still have a lot to learn about each other. A lot to learn." He stressed the last few words and that confused her. Henri reached out and took his wife by the hand.

Sonia took Matthew's hand and noticed a little look pass between him and his mother. She couldn't place what it meant, but it made her uneasy.

"Matthew, why don't you take Sonia on a tour of the house? I've put you in the guest quarters out back. I thought maybe you'd like some privacy."

"Good idea. I think we could do with a lay down."

"I should help your mother tidy away first."

"No need, you're a guest here Sonia. I know how hard you and Matthew work for Mr North. Please, this is your holiday. Rest and relax. Take the bottle of wine and glasses with you. I'll call when dinner is ready." Matthew's mother took her plate from her hands, and Matthew led her from the room. They got outside, and she dug her heels in.

"I was happy for you to keep whatever secrets you wanted till you thought you were robust enough to tell me but I will not sit in a room with a group of people who obviously know everything. That is disrespectful to not only me but also our relationship. I will not be made a fool of."

"Sonia, please. Give me time."

"We've been together for six months. What is it? Do you not trust me? I've told you everything there is to know about me. I've opened my heart, let it bleed truths. Now is the time, Matthew. Now or never. Your decision." She turned around and stomped towards the guest house without looking back to see if he was following.

CHAPTER TWENTY-TWO

Matthew

His world was shattering in front of him.

"Sonia." It was all he could say, and his voice wavered.

"Your choice Matthew. I'm going to lay down."

She slammed the door to the guest house, leaving him outside.

"Give her a few minutes to calm down and then go and tell her everything."

His father appeared beside him and placed his hand upon his shoulder.

"I don't know if I can."

"Do you love her?"

"More than anything."

"Then you can."

"What if she hates me?"

"You did nothing wrong, Matthew."

"Dad."

His father stopped him.

"You did nothing wrong. It was her choice. She made the decision to die. Not you."

"But I could have stopped it."

"I wasn't there, but I know when someone is determined to die, nothing will be able to stop them. You can't watch them twenty-four-seven."

"I should have done something."

"Matthew, she is the past. Sonia is the future. Don't lose her."

His father was right. He needed to face what he always tried to hide.

"Thanks, dad."

"No worries. Now go and sort everything before dinner.

If your mother's meal is spoilt, she'll be a nightmare for weeks."

"I will."

With rather hesitant steps he trudged towards the guest house.

"If you haven't come to talk to me, then you can turn around and go back the way you came." Sonia turned the water off, dropped the towel that encased her body and got into the bath. She didn't even look at him. He took a seat on the toilet. His long legs crossed in front of him and an arm resting on the cistern. To an external viewer, he may look relaxed, but he was far from it. Sonia looked over to him and then ducked under the water to wash her hair. When she surfaced, he'd finally managed to find his voice.

"I did many different assignments when I was in MI5 and also when I was seconded to MI6. I travelled to lots of different countries. I always returned home to England or came back here afterwards. I took time out and broke from the intensity that each assignment brought." He was staring in front of him, not really at anything, not even at Sonia. The chill of the memories surrounded him. This was why he hated to say anything, to go back to those places. Sonia thought his parents knew everything but the reality was he had never told a living soul all that happened on his last assignment. "I was given a commission by MI5 to Paris; it wasn't to be a short one. I was told from the outset that I could be there at least a few years. I had an American woman from the FBI as, my partner. I was given a new identity, Matthias Durand. The American agent was supposedly my wife, Jennifer. Jen as I called her. I'd left the south of France at a young age with my family and made my fortune and name in England and America as part of the Milieu or mafia branch there. I'd met Jennifer when she'd started working for my firm. We'd apparently fallen in love and married. I'd grew tired of the hatred for foreigners in England though; the discrimination only worsening. Especially when Jen was assaulted for being married to a Frenchman. We had left and moved to Paris to start afresh in a country which would welcome us both and our money. My task was simple, to infiltrate a particular section of the French mafia and help eliminate human trafficking in the UK and USA." He paused. He could vividly remember his first meeting with Francois LaFont, the leader of the Corsican gang of the same name. "We were able to get in, and I started off as a soldier but soon became a captain."

"After I became a captain, an opportunity came up that brought me in direct contact with the boss, Francois Lafont. I was his consigliere. It was the connection we needed, and I started to take the firm down from the inside."

"What about Jennifer? Or...what was her real name?"

"Beth."

"What about Beth?"

He sighed heavily. "Beth and I got close. Eventually, we became lovers. She inserted herself with the wives and girl-friends of the gang and used that to help with bringing them down. I had to travel to England for a deal and took her with me. We made an on the spot decision, went to Gretna Green, and were married." Sonia let out a pained breath. He tried to hold her again, but she stood, her hands held out in front of her.

"You're married?"

"No."

"Divorced?"

"No."

"Dead." The word caught in her throat.

He nodded.

"Oh God."

She put her hand over her mouth like she was going to be sick.

"Shortly before the assignment was due to end, Beth was lunching with LaFont's wife and several other women attached to the gang. The restaurant was attacked. LaFont's wife had her throat slit in front of everyone. Beth had a knife plunged into her stomach."

"She died because they thought they were killing the wife of the consigliere?"

"She didn't die from that attack."

"What? I don't understand."

"She did, later. Francois had a son, Jean-Claude. He had arranged the hit. He had told the attackers to kill his mother but only injure Beth."

"His own mother?"

"He knew it would weaken his father and make him vulnerable. What he didn't know-- Beth was carrying our child. The baby died, and she had a hysterectomy to save her life."

Sonia had tied him down to his story this far, kept him from falling deeply under the spell of his memories but no longer. He was back there the day of her death. The sounds and smells of the vibrant city of Paris invaded his nostrils as he looked around to see Beth's final moments.

"Are Jasper and the others on the way?" Beth moved slowly over the sculptured lawn of the LaFont mansion's gardens.

"They will be here within the hour. They have enough evidence to take down Francois and Jean-Claude. They will rot in prison forever."

"And we will go back to our regular lives."

"Isn't that what you want?"

"I don't think life will ever be normal for me again."

She held her hands over her stomach where stitches still marked the effects of the knife that had stolen their child.

"I love you, Beth. This changes nothing." He took her hands and kissed both of them before kneeling before her and kissing where the baby had grown.

"I'm not a proper woman anymore."

"You're all the woman that I need. Child or not. We will always be together."

"I should go see Francois. He wants me to help pick out clothing for his Elise's funeral dress."

"I'll come with you."

"No. There is no need. You go get everything ready for Jasper."

"I'll at least walk you in. Francois may be an awful man, but I can't deny how much he loved his wife. I owe him condolences for that.

"Five minutes. Then you go."

"Okay, bossy."

Matthew followed her into the house. Monsieur LaFont was sitting shrouded by the darkness of thick drapes in his grand sitting room. He looked like he hadn't slept in weeks not just days.

"Francois?" She cooed. He didn't answer. Just beckoned for her to come to his side. The old man looked directly at him.

"Matthias. You'll find who did this and bring them to me." Francois spoke in French, but the words entered his head in English.

"They will die painfully. You have my word on this."

"You're good. I'm glad that you're here with us. Even if it means suffering to your beautiful wife. When the funeral is over; take a break; go to Corsica. You can stay with my friends."

"That is very generous of you Francois." Beth placed a blanket around the old man's shoulders.

"I'm going to go and speak to my sources, see what I can find."

Francois took Beth's hand. "Let's go choose a dress for my wife."

"Au revoir, Matthias." Beth kissed his cheek.

Matthew watched them go.

"Matthias. Where's my father?" Jean-Claude called from the doorway.

Jean-Claude had always been a bit of a mystery to Matthew. He appeared loyal to the LaFont's, but there was always a question mark in his mind as to how far that allegiance ran.

"Do you know who did it yet?"

"Not yet but I'm working on it."

"Work quicker. I want answers by the end of the day."

"You'll have them." Just not the answers that he wanted.

"How is Jen? Should she be up and around already."

"She's stronger than she looks."

"I'm sorry she was involved."

"So am I for her sake and the baby."

"Baby?"

"She was pregnant."

"What?" Jean-Claude's face paled. "You hadn't said?"

"It was early stages."

"Fuck."

"That is putting it mildly."

"I should go check on my father." Suddenly the younger LaFont couldn't wait to get away from him. Matthew didn't care, though. His phone rang.

"You here?" His screen flashed up the code name for Jasper.

"Yes."

The next thing Matthew knew he was thrown through the air. A massive explosion ripped through the mansion in a violent crescendo of flames and flying debris. Hard stone rained down on him, bruising and bloodying his skin. He fought to remain conscious.

"Matthew?"

"Explosion." It was all he could manage as dust starting to settle all around him invaded his lungs. The coughing started.

"We'll be there in five minutes."

Matthew turned to look at what remained of the mansion. Nothing.

"Beth?" Was the last word he had managed before the darkness claimed him.

"Who was responsible? Jean-Claude was in there. It couldn't have been him."

Sonia was sitting right beside him now. She had a hold of

his hand.

"Beth did it."

"What?" She shook her head disbelievingly.

"I found out afterwards. She had rigged the mansion to explode. That day she took the detonator with her. She destroyed herself and Jean-Claude but allowed me to live."

"I'm so sorry Matthew."

"I've never told anyone as much as I've said today. James knows bits."

"You lost your wife and child in the space of a few days and in a violent manner. No wonder you've wanted to keep that buried so deep within you." She leant into him, her warmth surrounding his body. For once she was giving comfort, and he was taking it.

"The darkness is locked away where it can be controlled. If you let it out it destroys you. That's the reason I left Paris the day she died. My father dealt with the funeral. He hadn't even met Beth. He had her buried in a small graveyard near where we'd lived."

"Have you been there?"

"No."

"But you can't hide from what happened forever. You taught me that."

"I was never one to follow my own rules." He kissed the top of her head.

Sonia shifted on the bed so that her deep brown eyes looked up at him. "You forced me to confront my past, so we are going to do the same with you."

"What?"

"We are going to go to Paris so that you can say goodbye."

CHAPTER TWENTY-THREE

Sonia

"Do you know what plot she is in?" Sonia looked around at the old mementoes to those that had been lost to heaven. "No. I don't." Matthew looked down at his feet in shame. "It's ok." She squeezed his hand reassuringly. "I'll go and ask."

"Slight problem."

"What?"

"You don't speak French."

"Damn it. You go."

Matthew disappeared into the church. She took a seat on a bench to wait. Her eye was caught by a man watching them, his face was thunderous. Matthew re-appeared with a map, and the man was gone.

"The priest has marked the map."

They meandered through the rows of ornamental graves and sepulchres. Ornate crosses and angels decorated them all. A mournful lament came from behind a large stone carving. Sonia surmised the elderly woman she spied was mourning the loss of her husband. She, herself, had grown so close to Matthew that she could image herself doing the same should anything happen to him. She couldn't think about that, though. Everything he had told her had been a massive shock; it was an entirely different life that he had lived before he met her. But in many ways, it was what had defined the man that she had fallen in love with. It was responsible for his caring nature and the strength that he showed her. That first time he had knelt before her on the plane while she told him the story of her parents. That was who Matthew was as a result of his past. She never wanted him to change that.

"This is it." Matthew's voice broke her out of her reflection. She looked over at the grave in front of her. She'd been expecting to see the name Beth Carter, but her breath was taken away when she read, 'Jennifer Durand.'

He knelt in front of the grave and placed his hand on the soft earth that would have been at her feet. "She had no family. Nothing before the assignment. I never fully became Matthias Durand, but she did become Jennifer." He stood and turned away from the grave. "I don't think I should have come. I destroyed her life. She carried my child and lost the ability to have any more because of who I was."

"Stop." Sonia stepped forward and placed her hand on Matthew's chest. "You looked out for each other. You cared for each other. You were blessed with the child as a result. That child will be in heaven with its mother now. They will be caring for each other. Watching over you as you live your life and be the good guy that you are. Beth made her own decision to end things her way. She set you free because she knew what a good man you are."

"Sonia, please. I killed people while I was undercover. I helped with trafficking women."

"And you saved as many as you could." She bit back at his self-pity. "And you've continued to protect people. Beth sacrificed herself because you're one of the good guys that will always put others before himself."

"I should have protected her. That is what a husband does."

She pointed towards the grave. "You did. You gave her peace for eternity."

"But I didn't give her life."

"I don't know why Matthew, but she didn't want life. You couldn't have stopped her."

He slumped to the ground. A heavy sigh leaving his resigned lips.

"I couldn't have saved her."

Sonia shook her head.

Matthew made the sign of the cross while he repeated a

prayer in French. When he was done, he stood and held out his hand for her.

"Thank you."

"For what?"

"For making me come here. You were right. I should have followed my own advice years ago. I feel calmer already. She was a strong and brave woman who made a terrible sacrifice at a time where her emotions were destroyed. I'm lucky to have had her love even if it was such a short period."

He leant forward and gave her a kiss.

"You said something about the Eiffel Tower, didn't you?"

"I did."

Matthew turned back to the grave and took one last look, put his arm around her shoulders, and she nestled her head against his chest.

"I love you."

"I love you too."

The Eiffel tower loomed large before them, and Sonia craned her neck so she could look all the way to the top. The metal structure was a feat of modern engineering. They purchased their tickets and then travelled to the observation deck top. It was late in the day, and the eager tourists had already been, so it wasn't that crowded.

"Wow," That view is stunning," Sonia exclaimed as she looked about over the city of love. You can even see Sacre Coeur in the distance that way and Notre Dame over there.

"I've never been sure whether I prefer this view or the view from the London Eye."

"You've been on the London eye?"

"You haven't?"

"No."

"You live in London and have never been on it!"

" I've never been one to spend my money on frivolities."

"Actually, true. I didn't pay for my trip."

"James."

They both laughed, and she leant forward against the railings. A gust of evening wind blew around the top, and she shivered. Even though it was a hot day it was getting late in the day and they were high up. Matthew sensing her cold pulled the rucksack off his back and removed a long shawl she had put in there earlier. He wrapped it around her shoulders and then pressed the warmth of his body into hers. They were standing overlooking the Louvre. There were a couple of other tourists and a guard up with them.

"I'll be back in a minute."

Matthew walked over to the guard, and they conversed quietly. The guard walked over to the other tourists and started to engage with them by leading them off in the opposite direction of the tower to her and Matthew.

"What did you do?"

"You'll see. Turn around and admire the view. No sound whatsoever." Matthew said it in the tone that made shivers run down her spine. She obeyed and looked out back over the view of Paris. His hand circled around her breast. The nipple peaked instantly.

"Matthew." Her voice sounded a little panicked.

"Colour." His voice rumbled in her ear.

"Green." She was nervous, but no way in hell did she want him to stop.

"Part your legs sweetheart."

Her breath quickened with each step she took to comply. Matthew bunched up the bottom her of dress and delved underneath to flash across her already damp knickers. He pressed his body harder into hers, and she could feel his cock hardening against her bottom. She couldn't help but wiggle against it.

"Don't tempt me. I'm not able to fuck you here, but you'll get off."

With that, he slid a finger under her knickers and across her clit. Fuck, she was on fire. He worked his fingers over her slit and slid one inside her. She tried not to moan.

A second finger joined the first, and he angled his hand so he could rub her clit at the same time. Her eyes blurred, and she struggled to maintain the sense of where she was, the fire building between her thighs engulfing her. Matthew's voice growled into her ear.

"Come."

And she did. She exploded into a powerful orgasm there on the top of the Eiffel Tower. Her body shaking with waves of pleasure flooding through it. The scream formed in her throat and she slammed her head quickly into Matthew's shoulder and bit down on his t-shirt and flesh to muffle the noise.

The evil bastard actually chuckled.

.

CHAPTER TWENTY-FOUR

Matthew

After a couple more days in Paris spent exploring the sights it was time to return to Bordeaux. They didn't visit Jennifer's grave again despite Sonia asking Matthew if he wanted to. He'd stated that that part of his life was over and for the first time he felt it. There also hadn't been a public repeat of sexual deviance, although behind the bedroom door they had swung from the chandeliers in the hotel. James would be proud to know his precious antique lights had been used for such a purpose and the ceiling hadn't caved in. Sonia had had a fit of giggles when they had seen the dying slave statue of Michelangelo's in the Louvre. He'd later found out it was because of his small penis and she imagined the disappointment of his lovers. He guessed the old adage of it isn't the size, it's what you did with it was lost on his girlfriend. Although he was quietly intrigued by her suggestion, they could get a sculpture made of his for when he was away with James, so she didn't have to miss him too much.

"What time do we get back to Bordeaux?" Sonia put her hand over the copy of La Monde newspaper that he was reading.

"Vingt minute." His brain was so focused on reading in French that he answered the same. She just looked at him. "Twenty minutes."

"Time for a quickie in the toilets?"

"You're insatiable."

"You've brought out the sex goddess in me that loves a public place."

"Wait until later. I've got a better idea for a public place for you."

"Where?"

"You'll have to wait and see." He raised his eyebrow, and she pouted. "You know what that gets you."

"Well, not fucked in a train toilet that's for sure." He pulled his paper back up and she let out an exaggerated groan.

"What I have planned is much better."

Forty-five minutes later they were in the car speeding up the A10, her hand resting on his thigh as he drove. They hit a small road and travelled along it, the car bouncing around. Not the best for the suspension but the place where they were going was worth it. A medieval chateau appeared before them.

"Whoa." Sonia let out an astonished breath. "A Chateaux. Look at the turrets. It's stunning."

"And mine."

"What?" She spluttered out the word.

"James bought it for me. He's been helping me do it up so should I ever want to leave him I can retire here."

"It's yours." He could tell the words were still sinking in.

"Yes. In fact, it was actually another ancestral home. During the Revolution, it was taken away from us though and passed to Republicans. My family went the way of most aristocracy then and met the guillotine.

"I'm sorry. That must have been hard to find out, but at least you've got this back now."

"There was a lot of damage inside after World War II. You can still see some bullet marks on the walls from where a fight took place here. It's not had the best history, but I plan on changing that. Make it the seat of the Sawyer generations for years to come."

"Sawyer generations?"

"When the time is right." The thought of Sonia getting pregnant scared the life out of him at the moment, but there would come a time. "Work hasn't started inside yet, or I would have brought you here to stay, rather than go to my parents'."

He weaved his way around the building and led Sonia through a white stone arch into the garden. This was the part he wanted to show her, and this was the part where her sudden love of public display would come to fruition. "Remove your clothes."

"What?" Sonia went from admiring the gardens to open mouthed and staring at him in two seconds flat.

"I said remove your clothes, my little submissive."

"But your gardener?"

"Is not here today."

"Can anyone see us?"

"This from the lady who orgasmed at the top of the Eiffel tower." He rolled his eyes. "Last chance or I'm getting back into the car."

Sonia slowly began to remove her clothes and dropped them all onto the ground.

"Turn around. There is a little something else you need."

"Matthew?"

She arched her back when the first drop of suntan oil hit it.

"Can't have that beautiful skin of yours getting burnt now can we?" He rubbed the lotion into her skin, making her a little slippery. Part of his plan. He paid particular attention to her breasts and the shaved cleft between her legs. "Especially these parts."

"What happens now?"

"You run."

"What?"

"You run."

He slapped her backside and she took off over the green grass of the manicured lawn.

He waited a couple of seconds while removing his clothing before moving over the grass after her.

"Sonia." He called, his voice low and full of desire. She had disappeared into the forests surrounding the chateaux. "You know you can't hide from me. I can smell your need for me even from here."

He twisted and turned among the trees of the forest before he spotted her naked backside flash between the sturdy old wooden trunks. Silently he prowled, the scent of her need for him inveigling his nostrils.

"How do you like my hands between your thighs...strong and hard, or soft and gentle? You know I can get you off with just one look."

A streak of brown hair darted between the trees before him, and he sped, quickly towards it. He caught her and wrapped his arms around her body. Her slippery suntan oil caught him off guard the first time, and he lost his grip, but on the second time he managed to catch her and pulled her to the floor. His hands roamed over her body, searching out the seductive flesh he had so often marked as his own. She let out a wanton moan that went straight to his dick.

"You are mine, my love. Forever more."

Quickly flipping her onto her back he surged inside her, his rigid length pushing the boundaries of her tight haven so that she called out in ecstasy.

She was his. He thrust harder and harder while she lay upon the sun-warmed ground.

"Come for me, sweetheart."

He didn't need to ask her twice. On the final word she exploded. She was his present, his future and in many ways his past. She defined him. She surrounded him. She gave him everything that she was and nothing would ever change that. This was the future that he would always live. His cock buried deep inside the warmth that only this one woman could give him. He groaned a final release and collapsed upon her.

"I love you always." The decision had been made. His heart made it for him. Love. It was here. Digging into his heart like a vine surrounding a fence in its beautiful floral nature.

"I love you forever more."

They lay there, entwined, for what seemed like an eternity. His cock hardened again, and he took her again. This time more slowly, savouring every inch of her body. They didn't often make love like this, just simple in its pleasure. Frequently they 'kinked' it up because that's what they both enjoyed but here and now this felt right. The sun started to lower on the horizon, its glow turning beautiful hues of red, orange and pink.

*

It was almost dark by the time they pulled up the driveway of the winery. Flashing lights illuminated the night sky, Sonia looked toward him, her face paling.

"Matthew?" He put the car into park and automatically opened the door and got out. He didn't answer Sonia, he just needed to find out what was going on. His legs took him towards the police that were surrounding his family's home. He could sense Sonia running alongside him to keep up.

"Mama, Papa?" He called and the police turned to him. They barred the way.

"Mr Sawyer?" A portly gentleman stepped forward.

"Yes."

"I'm Inspector De Ternay. I'm afraid you can't go inside. There has been an incident."

It suddenly clicked in his brain that they were speaking French when Sonia wrapped her hand around his. "Can you speak English?"

The Inspector switched his language. "We were called an hour ago to reports of gunshots."

"No." Sonia's worried response caught in her throat.

"We are still trying to investigate what happened."

Matthew pushed past the gendarme sat in the doorway in one fluid motion. The door to the hallway opened, and he saw a medic working on a prone body on the floor. Blood flowed in a circle around the person. The medics stepped back and called the death. Sonia took hold of his hand again as the identity of the dead person was revealed. Guilt and relief washed over him; it was one of the farmhands and not his family. That guilt quickly turned to anger, a fierce rage that was directed at the inspector that had followed them.

"Where are my family?"

"Matthew?" He spun quickly around at his Aunt Lourdes' voice. She ran to him. Blood covered her cream shirt, she slammed her body into his, and he wrapped his arms around hers.

"What happened?"

"It was awful. So awful. He shot them." His aunt's voice broke. He knew he should be comforting her, but instead, he pushed her back and started to shake her.

"Shot who?"

Tears streamed down his aunt's cheeks.

"Your parents."

CHAPTER TWENTY-FIVE

Sonia

Shot.

The word rumbled around Sonia's head.

"Lourdes, where are they?"

Henri staggered into the room. "They are at the hospital. You need to take Matthew. Get him there quickly. He needs to be with them before..."

"What happened?"

He looked over to where the Inspector had his back to them now and then to Matthew. From his pocket, he withdrew a small box and handed it to her.

"What is this?"

"Get Matthew to his parents first. He needs to say goodbye. He'll know what to do after."

"What about the police?"

"There is nothing they can do. Go, Sonia. Please hurry. For Matthew's sake."

"Matthew. We have to go to the hospital, your mother and father are there."

"You drive."

Matthew's hand hovered over the doorknob. She could see he was willing himself to turn the handle. The door pushed open, and the beep of machines hit them first. Matthew's mother lay attached to a device. A bandage covered her head, and there was a stump where an arm had once been.

Matthew put his fist through the glass of the door.

"Matthew." She tried to comfort him.

"The box, what was in it."

With the worry over his parents, she had forgotten the

box.

"I don't know. I haven't looked."

"Give it to me." He growled the words, not with any passionate intentions, she was used to that particular noise coming out of his mouth, but with pure venom.

"Mr Sawyer?" A man in scrubs interrupted them. "I'm the doctor who has been looking after your parents."

"Where is my father?"

"He is in recovery. We will have him brought down here soon. He is critical. The next few hours will let us know more. At present, I can only give you a fifty-fifty chance of survival for both your parents. To be honest, with the wounds they had, they are lucky to be alive now."

"My mother's arm?"

"She was shot twice in it. I'm sorry. There was just no way we could save it. Your mother was also hit over the head, hence the bandage, but Mr Sawyer, I must tell you. Your father was shot in the head. I can give you no guarantees of what will happen, if and I remind you that's a very big if, he wakes."

Sonia brought her hand to her mouth to try to keep quiet the cry that was threatening to leave her lips. She had to be strong for Matthew now. She couldn't think of the suffering that his parents must have experienced. She had to focus on keeping Matthew all together and not allowing him to lose his sense of control. He was a trained killer. This could end badly.

"I want my father in the same room as my mother. If this room isn't big enough, find one. I will pay whatever you need."

"We will see to it at once. There is nothing you can do for now, I would suggest you get some rest, but if you want to stay, I'll have a nurse bring you some drink and clean clothes."

Matthew turned away from the doctor and pulled his phone out. The doctor was dismissed. The doctor left them alone in the room, and she took a seat next to Matthew.

"The box." His voice was far too controlled; it was scaring her so much.

She gave it to him and watched as he opened it. Inside were two rings and a crest. The crest bore a furred Phoenix holding a fleur de Lis with the writing Vincit Omnia Veritas' below it.

"Truth conquers all things." Matthew shut his eyes. "Did my aunt and uncle say anything about the man that did this?"

"No."

"These are my wedding rings. I didn't wear mine. Jennifer had it around her neck. They were never found after the explosion."

He pulled out his phone and dialled. The phone was on speaker.

"Where are you?"

"Outside the hospital." Jasper's voice answered.

"We're in room two four five."

Matthew hung up. "You have to leave. Jasper will take you."

"What?" She scraped her chair back and stood up. "I'm not going anywhere; I'm staying right by your side."

"You need to get back to England and into safe custody. You have to do whatever Jasper says."

Jasper came through the door. "I'm so sorry. I got here as soon as we got the alert from your parents."

"Is it him?"

"From the description your uncle gave to the gendarmes and the fact they are backing off the investigation, I would say so."

"Have you got everything in place for Sonia?"

"Yes. I've got a car outside, and the airfield is nearby."

"Good, I want guards put on this door. I've asked for mum and dad to be kept together."

"Already in place. They came with me."

"Ok, take her. Keep her safe for me." Matthew sat back down at his mother's bedside and took the hand that was still there into his.

"You're not coming?"

"Neither of us are going anywhere." She sat down next to Matthew and folded her arms across her chest.

Jasper raised an eyebrow towards Matthew.

"Pick her up and carry her. Watch her left leg, though, she looks to go straight for the balls." Matthew spoke without even taking his eyes off his mother.

"What the fuck!" She spat the words out, Jasper took a step nearer to her. "Come any closer, and they will be needing a third hospital bed in here, and if you don't stop shutting me out Matthew Sawyer and giving me answers, then they may as well add a fourth."

"Shall I wait outside?" Jasper had stopped advancing and looked towards Matthew. Sensible man, she would render him unable to breed for the foreseeable future if he tried anything.

"No, it's okay, I should have known she would be this stubborn."

"I'm not stubborn, I'm trying to care for the man I love. Although I'm seriously starting to wonder if the words he spoke to me this afternoon were all a bunch of lies."

Jasper withdrew to the corner of the room, and Matthew got to his knees in front of her.

"I'm sorry. Sonia, I love you, and I'm scared. I am facing the possibility that my mum and dad are going to die and if I don't get you into protective custody, he'll find you and try the same thing."

"Who will find me? Please, I need to know so that I can protect myself."

He took a deep breath.

"Jean-Claude."

"But he died in the explosion?"

"That is what we were led to believe. Please, I need you to go with Jasper and get back to England. He'll make sure you're safe while my former colleagues try to find Jean-Claude and bring him down."

"What about you?"

"I can't leave my parents."

"Let me stay the night. You said there were guards outside the door. Nobody will get in here."

"I can't, I need to know you're safe to be strong. Please, sweetheart, go with Jasper."

"I don't want to leave you. What if he comes for you? I can help you fight. I can't lose you."

"You won't. You'll see. You'll wake up in the morning, and I'll be there beside you in the bed. My parents will be under armed guard and recovering." It was easy to see that he was trying to reassure himself.

"I want to know the second your parents wake or Jean-Claude is caught so I can come back here."

"I promise. Jasper will stay with you the entire time."

"I love you."

"We need to get going if we're going to make our flight clearance." Jasper interrupted.

"Okay." She pushed herself out of the chair and took hold of Matthew's hand. He came with her to the door and then let go; she walked out. She turned around to see him take a look at her before closing the door. There was too much finality here. She could almost feel her heart breaking. He wasn't leaving her, but she wondered if she would see him again.

"Matthew isn't going to be a part of the investigation is he?"

"He'll be at the hospital under our protection."

"And when Jean-Claude is caught?"

Jasper slammed the door shut. He climbed in the other side.

"Jasper?"

"Please don't ask me that question again."

"He won't be the same man when I see him again will he?"

"I think you should prepare yourself for the worse."

Jasper pressed a button on his wheel, and a call started

ringing before she answered.

"We'll be there in a few minutes. Start the engines."

"I'll be ready."

From out of nowhere, a car skidded to a halt in front of them. Jasper swerved, but they clipped it, which sent the car into a spin. It flipped, rolled, and slammed to a halt against a grove of trees. Her head bumped hard against the dashboard. Jasper groaned beside her, and she looked over to see him hanging from his seatbelt. Smashed glass littered his side of the car where the window had broken. His face was covered in little cuts. They needed to get out of the car. She released her seat belt and fell onto the roof of the car. Her body ached from the force of the impact.

"Jasper. We need to get out." She tried to release his seatbelt, but it was stuck. He groaned again but didn't stir.

Jean-Claude was coming for her. She needed to think. Jasper must have a gun. The door behind her was ripped open, and large hands grabbed hold of her legs and started to pull. She tried to find something to anchor herself to, but nothing helped, she was pulled cleanly from the car and onto her knees before an imposing dark haired man.

"Jean-Claude."

CHAPTER TWENTY-SIX

Matthew

It seemed like days since his mother and father had been placed side by side in the hospital room. It had only been a few hours though. His phone rang. He answered it without looking at the caller ID.

"Hey, sweetheart."

"I didn't know you cared that much." He heard a scuffle over the phone.

"Matthew." Sonia's voice.

"I don't care how you get there, but meet me where this all started. You have three hours."

"I'll be there. You hurt her, and I won't be responsible for what I do to you."

"Matthew, don't come. Stay with your parents. You know it's a trap."

A hard slap resonated through the phone.

"Shut the fuck up bitch."

"Go to hell." He heard his woman spit at Jean-Claude.

"Sonia, sweetheart. Try to leave something left of the man for me to beat on please."

"I'm not making any promises." They both chuckled despite the intensity of the situation.

"That's enough." Matthew heard Sonia scream. Jean-Claude had obviously pulled her away from the phone again. "You've three hours Matthew. Don't waste them."

The line went dead.

Jasper appeared at the door. Dried blood had formed a clump over his eye. Matthew prowled forward and smacked his fist hard into his friend's jaw. The agent stumbled backwards against the wall. Matthew stormed out of the room.

"Are you going to tell me where you're going?"

"What do you think?"

"You know doing this alone is suicide."

"If Sonia dies, I've got nothing left to live for."

"She isn't Beth."

"No, she's not."

"We'll follow discreetly. The first sign of trouble, and I'm giving the order to go in after you."

"Nobody kills him but me."

"I'll give you that."

"Give me your gun."

"Please."

"Give me your gun, or I'll punch you in the face again."

"You always were so polite."

"I'll never change."

Jasper handed him the gun, and he placed it into the back of his trousers.

"Bullets."

Jasper handed over a few clips.

"I've seen you shoot before. You only need the one. Don't get dead, Matthew."

"I don't plan on it."

With a deep breath, he strode purposefully from the hospital. Clicked the keys to his car and climbed in. This would end today, with Jean-Claude La Font suffering.

CHAPTER TWENTY-SEVEN

Sonia

"Hey, I need to pee." Sonia shifted in her chair and glared at Jean-Claude.

"Merde, Pierre. Take her."

The heavyset man with a face like a pit bull stood up.

"My pleasure." Pit-bull un-cuffed her from the chair.

"You want to wet yourself instead then be my guest. I like it when little girls do that right before I fuck them. Shows them just who their Papa is."

"Pierre. Just take the bitch to the bathroom. I need to concentrate on this." Jean-Claude was losing his temper as the time for Matthew to arrive approached. This was good. If she could play on that stress, she could force him into making errors.

"Come on bitch." Pit-bull pushed her into the small bathroom--a hole in the ground like many public French toilets.

She gave him a death stare. "Turn around."

"What, so you can bash me on the head? I don't think so."

"And there was me hoping to get a better view of your cute backside." She gave him a wink and subtly pushed her breasts together.

"Nice try."

"Damn, and there was me thinking that you had the brain of the ugly dog you look like." He slammed her up against the wall; his hand around her throat.

"I guess you never got the memo."

"What memo?"

"Never get me in a position where I can connect my left leg with your balls." With a swift knee-jerk, she slammed hard into his groin. Pit-bull let out an agonised scream and fell to the floor. She slammed her foot into his face, knocking him out cold and breaking his nose for probably the third time. Then she made a run for it.

The commotion behind her told her Jean-Claude was after her. She jerked to the right and behind a pillar. Silently she waited for them to run past and outside looking for her but they never came.

She held her breath and silently tried to creep closer towards the door. This would be so much easier if she had a weapon. She had nearly made it to the door when it opened, and Matthew walked in.

"Run," was all she managed before taking off towards the door again. Matthew was right behind her, his hand reaching inside his trousers to take his gun out. A shot fired, and Matthew stopped; his leg gave way.

"Matthew." She stopped running and came to his side.

"Go."

"You know that isn't going to happen."

It was too late. Jean-Claude and his associates were upon them and surrounded them.

"Nice of you to join us, Mr Sawyer."

"Pierre." Pit-bull appeared with blood caked all over his nose, he snarled towards her. "Why don't you take Miss Anderson and tie her up again. This time try not to let her hit you in the balls."

"Get the fuck off me." She screamed and tried to kick out. Jean-Claude stepped forward and straight onto Matthew's leg where he had been shot. He reluctantly let out a yell of pain.

"Shut up bitch and do as you're told."

He stepped off Matthew's leg only when she became placid and allowed herself to be led back to the room. Turning back to see what was going to happen next to her lover, she watched in horror as Jean-Claude took the gun and whacked it hard over Matthew's head knocking him unconscious.

"No!" She screamed so loud that Jean-Claude looked at

her. His lip snarled upwards in an evil motion that sent shivers through her body. It was a look she had only seen once before, and that was the night her mother died. That night was fuelled by alcohol and poor decisions, though. What was happening right now was the direct result of a man that Wouldn't stop until she and Matthew were begging for mercy. He stepped forward towards her and grabbed her by the chin.

"Strip them and tie them both up naked. It's time they both learned some truths."

CHAPTER TWENTY-EIGHT

Matthew

His head hurt like a bugger and his leg wasn't much better.

"Well, it is nice of you to join us."

Matthew just kept his attention squarely focused on Sonia in front of him. She was shaking.

"I see you're just as delusional as my father if you think you're going to get out of this. Your life will end here today and this un-classy bitch that you call a girlfriend will be joining you as you rot in hell."

"We won't be the ones rotting in hell. We'll be off happily living our life." This time Sonia spoke, her eyes flooded with darkness, she'd regained her composure and strength from knowing that he was near.

Jean-Claude pulled her hair tight, her head pulled backwards. Matthew pulled at the ropes binding him, furiously trying to rip them so that he could wrap his bare hands around the man's throat till his eye popped out of his head.

Sonia spat into Jean-Claude's face. He had been right above her so that she could see the gloating on his face. In one quick swipe the Frenchman hit her square across the face sending her chair flying onto the floor.

"Fucking bitch." Jean-Claude kicked her in the stomach and she let out a pained scream.

He couldn't watch anymore.

"Are you so much of a coward? Why don't you untie me, and we can sort this man to man?"

"You think I'm scared of you?" Jean-Claude was facing him now. "You were a fool back then and you're a fool now."

"A fool, I'm not the one that had my mother's throat

slit." He fired back an insult that he knew would rattle.

"She deserved it, she never supported me over him. I would still be running stupid little errands if my mother and father had had their way. Giving all the top jobs to a bloody spy and then wondering why they kept going wrong."

"They gave you the crap jobs because you were no good at the important stuff. It took a real man to do that."

"What just like it took a real man to get your wife pregnant."

"Jean-Claude." It couldn't be. "Now that's no way to talk to my husband, in it?"

"Beth."

The slender form of his wife appeared in front of him, he could barely look at her, gone was the sweet catholic girl he had known, she was replaced by a gangster's wife dripping in the finest jewellery, designer clothing and coiffured hair.

"No, I chose the right side. It just took me a while." Jean-Claude wrapped his arms around her waist. Any love or remorse for her death that he once had sat like a putrid wound in the pits of his stomach.

"Who were the other two in the explosion."

"Who cares." Jean-Claude replied with a nasty sneer. "They did their job."

"At least the lady got a proper burial."

"Not that you would know. The other day was the first time you'd even been to my grave."

Sonia gasped.

"The man staring at me. It was you."

"You led me right to him. Pierre, why don't you sit Miss Anderson up. I want to have some fun." Before he could prepare himself Matthew found his stomach clenching up in agony when Jean-Claude swung a fist into it. The pain ripped through him but he refused to let out a noise, he was almost biting down on his tongue to show nothing. That was one of the first things he had taught for situations like this. Give nothing away. Show no pain less it shows a weakness. An ugly looking man with an obvious broken nose had righted Sonia in her chair. He punched her in the stomach; she was prepared and didn't even flinch. She definitely was his girl.

"Seems the woman is better at this than you."

"Well he always was a bit of a girl, I always used to beat him in training." Beth had taken a seat, her long legs crossed showing off her Jimmy Choo shoes.

"I'm not going to play your games Beth, so don't even bother trying. And dickhead," He faced the guy that had punched Sonia. "You hit her again and I'm going to break most of the bones in your body before I put you out of your misery permanently."

The bastard dared to do it again. He took a deep breath, calming himself. The time would come.

His eyes narrowed to slits when Jean-Claude picked up a bat. This wasn't good. Sonia may be able to withstand punches from a hand but with a bat. It would break every bone in her delicate little body. He needed to protect her. Meeting her apprehensive look, he calmly gave her reassurance, hope, the knowledge that help was on its way.

"Why him, Beth?" He turned to look at the woman he had thought dead.

"He is going places."

"What prison?"

"You know that will never happen. They couldn't capture me before and they won't capture me now." Jean-Claude was far too certain of his own name. He was going to enjoy wiping the smile off his face.

"We've followed your career, Matthew. You caused a lot of damage. I think when the news of your violent death comes out there will be a lot of people that are only too happy with it." Beth was like a changed woman. He couldn't believe that he once loved her. She had none of Sonia's class and warmth.

Broken nose man punched Sonia in the face. Jean-Claude reached for a bat on a nearby table and swung it hard into his stomach. He'd had time to clench but it still hurt. He did it twice more and Matthew heard the crack of his ribs breaking. He tried to keep his focus squarely on Sonia but the anger inside of him flared when he saw broken nose man rub his hands over her breasts. He was heading lower; no man would touch his girl that way. They hadn't tied his legs down so he kicked out. Without shoes on it wouldn't cause much damage but he had strength and the man collapsed to the floor.

"That was stupid." Jean-Claude swung the bat again, straight into his balls. A low blow that had his eyes watering and his brain failing to hold in the scream.

Sonia kicked out, catching Jean-Claude.

"That was a big mistake, bitch." Matthew summoned all the strength he could and strained against the ropes. They didn't give but the chairs weren't made of the stuff that could withstand a 6 foot 5 giant in a berserker fury and the back of the chair shattered. The wooden splinters fragmenting all across the floor. His hands were still tied but he could move. He head-butted Jean-Claude, who stumbled backwards. Beth screamed and lunged for him, a knife in her hand. He deflected her first thrust, but her second caught him and ripped through the flesh of his shoulder.

***

She was free.

Matthew was still holding his own with Beth and Jean-Claude, but the wound to his shoulder wept blood and it wouldn't be long before he needed help.

"Told you I'd get to fuck you in the end. I'm going to enjoy this." Pit-bull slammed into her, knocking her to the floor. He squeezed her breast. Stupid man. She'd kneed him once in the face and he hadn't learned anything. When her knee met his balls she sniggered at the shocked expression on his face. She rolled out from underneath him and grabbed a jagged piece of the broken chair. He jumped to his feet and lunged for her again, but before he knew what was happening she thrust the piece of wood directly into his stomach. He gurgled and blood came from his mouth. She spun to face Matthew just as Beth sunk the knife deep into the cavity of his clavicle.

***

The pain was excruciating. He struggled to maintain consciousness. The world spun, but Sonia was at his side and removing the bindings at his wrists. He pulled the knife out of his shattered clavicle with a sucking noise. He would only have one arm to fight with but that was better than none. Turning the knife around he struck a line down Jean-Claude's face. He swung the bat out in retaliation but both he and Sonia jumped back in time. Sonia was on the attack this time and managed to knock the smug smile off Beth's face when she caught the side of her face with the chair leg she held as a weapon. It ripped off the lower half of his wife's ear and sent her no doubt expensive earring flying across the room.

"I'll find that after you're dead and pawn it to pay for the next grave stone. Believe me, it won't be as flash and respectful this time."

"How does it feel knowing that you're sleeping with a married man. That I'm the reason he wouldn't marry you because he still loved me." Beth covered her ear but still rolled off a load of venom.

"I think still loved you is the optimum word. Sonia is about fifty times the woman you were. And a loads better submissive as well."

"Thank you handsome." Sonia advanced forward again, so did he.

"Maybe you're just a crap Dom. Ever thought of that Matthew. Too wrapped up in saving the world when it doesn't need saving." Jean-Claude aimed for his damaged shoulder and the pain of the bat connecting with the broken bone caused him to bend and vomit all over the floor. Sonia flipped over Beth and smacked the chair leg over Jean-Claude's head but Beth was just as quick and had another knife pulled out and sunk into Sonia's leg. She cried out and struggled to stay on her feet. They were losing this battle fast. If they didn't do something soon then they would die. Jasper must be here now. He needed to get a sign out to him. Jean-Claude came at him again but he caught his arm and thrust his head straight into the wall.

"Jean." Beth called out, Matthew rounded on the battered faced Frenchman to try and slam him into the wall again but he was too slow and Jean-Claude took his feet out from under him and sent him sprawling onto the floor. He kicked out and sent Jean-Claude to the floor this time and leapt to his feet in an elaborate back arc. That's when he saw it. The window. He looked to where Sonia was still in arm to arm combat with Beth. She was holding her own despite the fact her left leg was weak. Jean-Claude was still down so he made a beeline for the window. Wooden boxes where piled up next to it. With dwindling strength and a hell of a lot of pain, he picked one up and threw it through the window.

"You know she came to me after you two had fucked. Completely unsatisfied and needing me inside her showing her what a real man could do."

"You don't get it do you? She'll cast you aside when the next person comes along."

"She helped kill my father so I could take over. She has supported me all these years and I've supported her."

"She had you kill a baby that could have been yours."

"She made a sacrifice for the sake of the future."

"She has been playing you all along."

"She loves me."

They were circling each other now. Matthew turned and caught Jean-Claude off guard. With his damaged arm screaming at him to stop, he flipped Jean-Claude over his back and out of the window. He landed with a thud on the ground. His body jerking as the last embers of life left it. It was a shame he had died so easily. Matthew had wanted to make it painful.

Matthew turned to see Beth stab the knife through Sonia's body. She fell to the floor.

"No." He rushed for them, jumping straight at Beth. She was startled and couldn't escape him. He had her by the throat. His bare hands tightening around the tiny column that was her neck.

"You bitch. I'm going to drain every inch of your life to make sure that you're definitely dead this time."

"You don't have the guts to do that. You were always weak and self-sacrificing. Besides you forgot Jean-Claude."

"What the Jean-Claude that I just threw out of a window."

He had to give her some credit, a look of grief crossed her face for a second.

"Doesn't matter. His replacement is already lined up. And with you dead, I don't have to keep putting off a proposal this time."

Jasper burst in, gun's cocked and ready to fire.

"Beth." Jasper's face turned white. "What the..."

Before anyone else could move, Beth had a knife at his throat and began to press. Time seemed to pass so slowly.

He felt nothing though. No pain. Surely he should be gargling his last breath. Why was he not dying? Beth went limp. Sonia. She was standing holding a knife in Beth's heart. She stumbled, and he grabbed her. She tried to speak but nothing came out. Sonia collapsed. He couldn't move. He was frozen to the spot. He saw people mobbing around him. One checking on Beth, the other on Sonia. He heard the words alive coming from the man checking Sonia. He wanted to kneel down and help the medic who had rushed in but he couldn't. A blanket was thrown around him, the weight of it sending sparks through the knife wound to his clavicle. He couldn't breathe. He had to get out of here. He staggered in a weaving pattern towards the door. Jasper came up beside him and wrapped a supporting arm around.

"Let's get you to a medic."

"No."

"I'm not taking no for an answer."

"Okay. But not here. I need to disappear."

"Sonia's alive, man."

"I know. But she is injured. My dad could be dead and my mum lost her arm. It's all because of the decisions I made. I need to leave."

"You sure?"

"Yes."

CHAPTER TWENTY-NINE

Sonia

"I say we go with the blue petunia theme."

"Petunia's are so 2016."

"I agree; Mayfair have gone with Gerbera's. They look fabulous in contrast with the white backgrounds that they have used."

"But they don't last that long. We need our display to be the best. We need to get this title back again."

"Sonia what about you? Do you have any ideas?" Miranda turned to face her. The warming smile on James' mothers face had her searching her brain for an answer. She didn't know anything about flowers for goodness sake; let alone how to turn them into an award-winning display for a late summer fair. The fields of sunflowers that she had seen in France filled her memory. The ever-present tears of late started to well in her eyes.

"I don't know much about flowers, but in France they had fields of sunflowers. They looked so very pretty."

Miranda smiled and brought her attention back to her friends. "That could work, you know. The yellow and the black plus there are so many other varieties now. We could use it like a sunset."

"That is a brilliant idea."

"Oh, I like the sunset theme."

The women's voices faded out as she retreated inside her head. Ever since Matthew had disappeared she had lived there. James had flown to France later that day and brought her back to England when she was fit enough to travel. She had asked him to take her to see Matthew's parents before they left but he felt the journey would be too much for her. Instead he had set up a Skype call with them.

Eleanore was doing well and adjusting to having only one arm. Phillip had eventually come out of his coma. He was alive but struggling with memory loss and his speech had been affected. He was fighting it, though. Henri and Loudres were doing everything possible to keep the winery running smoothly for the family. When she was fully recovered from the stab wound to her stomach, Sonia was adamant that she was going to travel back to Bordeaux to see them.

James had brought her back to his home in Kensington and had installed her as a house guest to be mothered by Miranda as much as possible until she decided what she wanted to do next. Her job was there if she wanted it. He would never take it away from her. All she could think about though was Matthew.

She got to her feet and informed Miranda she was going to lay down as she was tired. Miranda nodded and offered to assist her to the bedroom but she refused. Her wound was heeling well but sometimes it still pulled a little when she moved quickly or stretched.

"Sonia." James called out when she walked pass his office. "The flower discussion is getting a little heated."

"Just a little. I'm afraid that I'm not really a flower person."

"I have to agree there. I leave that sort of thing to my mother." He chuckled. "How are you feeling?"

"Getting better. I was thinking maybe I should start looking for somewhere to live. Right now, I'm not sure I want to go back into being a bodyguard." At the moment all she wanted to do was curl up in a little ball and lay there. Not knowing where Matthew was, was killing her. Was he even alive? He'd had some pretty bad wounds. They could have got infected or he could have bled out. She'd been told he left with Jasper but she had no way of contacting him, short of storming down the Agency's door and demanding he speak to her. She didn't think that would get her very far though and would probably land her in jail more than anything.

"Why do you want to move out? You have your own room here."

"I have Matthew's room."

"It is your room as well."

"I'm sure he will come back soon and he's made it perfectly clear that he doesn't want me in his life anymore."

"Have you spoken to him, then?" James, who had been sitting at his desk, now stood and came around to perch on the front of it beside her. His long muscular legs crossed at the ankles. He wasn't her Dom, he was her boss, but he still gave off those vibes that made her shiver with a need to do as she was told.

"No. I haven't." She put her head down like a naughty school girl.

"Then how do you know he doesn't want you in his life anymore?"

"He left me."

"No, he took the coward's way to try to sort out his head. His father and mother had been shot. He didn't know if his father was still alive or not. His mother had lost an arm. You had been taken, and he had to watch guys strip you naked, touch you, hit you and stab you. Then, to top it all off, his wife that he thought was dead reappeared and tried to kill him. He lost his mind, I'm sure the blood loss he was experiencing didn't help that. He'll find it again and be back. Matthew has always been a tower of strength since the first day I met him. He rigidly controls everything. Do you know in MI5 his nickname was 'The Machine'? Because he never faltered, he never failed, he never showed he was human. What he's done, taking the cowards route--it shows that he is a human after all."

"You've spoken to him?"

"No, I have not. I have a private investigator searching for him, but Matthew is trained by MI5. If he doesn't want to be found just yet, then he won't be."

"Have you tried, Jasper?"

"Jasper is loyal to Matthew. I'll not get an answer from him."

"So we are none the wiser to where he is." Her heart deflated.

"But I'm not going to give up."

"Thank you for trying."

"Look, I think we both need a little bit of fun. Why don't we go to the club? You don't have to participate in anything. They have a demonstration night next week. We can go and watch."

"I don't know." She knew that James wouldn't try anything with her. She was Matthew's submissive to him and always would be. He would be like a protector. She couldn't hide away all the time. It wouldn't do her any good. She was just getting into a deeper and deeper mourning for the loss of her future.

"I'll try. I can't promise anything, though."

"That's all you can do." James placed his hand on her shoulder. "Sonia, I know what you are going through. I can't believe Amy isn't in my life. Every day, I want to run screaming through the streets, find her and carry her back here and fuck her till she sees sense and tells me she loves me. But she used her safe word with me. I need to give her time. If we are meant to be together, then we will be brought back together. Damn fate and all that. Matthew didn't use his safe word but his walking away means he needs space. I know that it is so incredibly hard for you, because it is virtually impossible for me, but you need to give him time."

"What if time doesn't heal him? What if he loses the love he has for me?"

"Then you'll deal with it because you are a strong woman. You can survive this."

"It hurts so much." She tried to stifle the tears that were now threatening to swamp her.

"I know." He pulled her into his arms and his warmth gave her some comfort. "Look. I'm not in the mood for working. I say we order pizza, ice cream and wine. Put on soppy movies and watch till we pass out?"

"Isn't that what girls do when they are miserable?"

"I hate to point this out but you are a girl."

"That is a nasty rumour I'll thank you not to repeat." A little chuckle left her lips.

"That's better."

"It happens occasionally."

"Just not when my mother and her cronies are talking about flowers."

"Yeah, that was a little tedious. I'm not really a lady that does lunch."

"Alright. We will go to the gym and lift weights like men, come back, and cry into our ice cream. How does that sound?"

"Perfect!"

CHAPTER THIRTY

Matthew

She looked so happy. Couldn't have been missing him at all.

Who was he kidding?

He could see the sadness behind her eyes as she followed behind Miranda towards the house. He'd been in hiding for weeks now recovering from his injuries. His arm was still in a sling, the broken bone in his clavicle healing nicely but slowly. The slash down his back had melded together and the stitches were starting to dissolve. Yes, his body was healing well. His mind, however, was still full of torment.

His wife, believed dead for so long, had reappeared and tried to kill him.

The last few years of his life had been a lie.

But the woman he now watched hadn't been, she had been the truth and he had walked away from her when he should have held her hand and reminded her he loved her. He didn't deserve her. He'd hurt her.

He needed to get out of here. He held his uninjured arm up for a taxi but it drove straight past when an Aston Martin pulled up beside him. It was a car he knew well. The door opened.

"Get in." James spoke, his face lined with concern. "If you don't, I will back up and drive forward again to break both your legs so I can get you in the car."

"You know I can still beat you with just one arm?"

"In your dreams. It's why I hired you, I'm too lethal with my bare hands."

"Good to see you have your humour back."

"Well one of us has to make jokes, or we are just annoying, slightly aging men." His boss laughed at him; Matthew knew he had no choice but to get in the car.

"How long have you known I was back in London?"

"My sources called me the second you caught the train at Paris. I was going to give you a week to contact us, and then I was going to storm down the door of your Mayfair hotel. I own the building, so don't think I wouldn't."

"It's why I chose your hotel. It would be the kick up the arse I needed if I didn't come and see you of my own accord."

"Plus you knew you'd never have to actually pay the bill."

"Well, that helped."

"Although I'm considering deduction of the mini bar expense from your wages. I think the hotel sold out of whiskey."

"Helps me sleep."

"I don't have to tell you that Sonia should be helping you recover."

"I know."

"Then why did you walk away."

"Because I was a complete idiot."

"No, you just proved you are mortal after all. I think I like you better for it."

James put his foot down on the accelerator and weaved through the traffic. Eventually he pulled into Kensington Park and put the car in neutral.

"What are you going to do about it?"

"What do you mean?"

"That girl is barely holding on. She doesn't even know if you are alive or dead. She put all her trust in you, and you shut the door to her. You're her Dom for god's sake. You may have broken the link between you forever."

Matthew shrugged. "I should have known I wouldn't get any sympathy from you."

"You're lucky I'm not kicking your arse for what you did. I understand that you got messed up but we talk through these things. You hurt me as well, man, disappearing like that. Come on. We are like brothers."

During his time away, Matthew had wallowed in guilt. He'd never loved Beth, not as much as he loved Sonia. When he saw Beth stabbing Sonia, and her lifeless body fall to the floor, it had destroyed something within him. At that moment in time he felt failure, like he had not protected the greatest person in his life. The one that had made him the man he was. He couldn't breathe. He couldn't think straight. All his brain had told him was to run.

As time had gone on, he knew Sonia would be angry at him, and he found it harder and harder to return. But he had to see her. He had to know how she was. Had he deliberately made himself visible to James so that he could end the nightmare of his own making?

He smelt like a bloody whiskey distillery, he couldn't remember the last time he had shaved. He was turning into the man of Sonia's nightmare. The man that he had helped her see wasn't a demon but weak. Weak, that was exactly what he was.

"I know it doesn't help, but I'm sorry."

"You're coming back?"

"I guess that depends on Sonia. I'm not going to make her life more difficult. She loves this job, and if she doesn't want me in her life, I'm not going to take it away from her. I'll make sure you are adequately covered though."

"That sounds like you are giving up and not even going to fight for the woman."

"I honestly don't know if I can fight for her. I did the one thing I promised I would never do to her."

"How far are you prepared to go to try?"

"Why?"

"Because I have a plan."

Matthew shifted uncomfortably in his seat. That expression on his boss's face could be scary. He didn't make billions without being a genius at the art of manipulation.

"Are you going to let me into this plan?"

"Soon. All you need to know for now is to be at the club on Thursday

CHAPTER THIRTY-ONE

Sonia

The bustier looked all wrong. With Matthew, he always adjusted it so it showed off her breasts to the best her athletic body could show them. When she put it on, it just looked wrong.

Jesus, why was she even going to the club with James. Would he expect her to scene with him? Maybe they should scene together. It would give them both the dominant/submissive pleasure they needed.

This was just crazy.

Matthew was just a man. One man.

And she missed him so much. The bedroom seemed so big without him. Argh! She needed to get a grip. She was one of those wimpy women she always vowed she wouldn't be. She was going to go to the club with James, and if he wouldn't scene with her, then she would find someone who was willing. She was attractive if she kept her trousers on so nobody could see the scars. She flinched, Matthew would give her ten lashes with a whip for that thought. She was pretty; she was beautiful; she was so fucking sexy he nearly came in his pants when she walked into a room. It had all been lies. Great big fat, ugly lies. She picked up her bag and threw it at the door just as James opened it. It hit him square in the face.

"Er...sorry." She bit her lip and looking guiltily at the floor.

"No, I'm sorry. I was knocking for a while, and when you didn't answer, I got worried. I shouldn't have barged in."

She'd been so lost in her thoughts that she hadn't even heard him.

"It's ok, I'm..."

"Do I need to give you ten lashes like Matthew would for doubting you look good? I prefer blondes, as you know, but you look beautiful."

"Do I really look alright?" She did a little twirl for him.

"May I do something?"

"What?"

He went to her cupboard and pulled out a short skirt. It was frilly, teal and black lace. Matthew had brought it for her. It was her favourite. Why did he have to pick that out?

"I want you to wear this."

"Boss." She hesitated, her hand over the skirt.

"Tonight you will call me James or Master when in the club. I'm not your boss. If you want to scene, and you cannot find a partner, which will not happen, then we can discuss it. We will have certain proviso's put in for both of us to ensure we're happy."

"Do I have to wear the skirt?" "You don't have to, but I honestly think it suits you."

"Ok, I'll wear it."

She changed, and they headed for the club.

She stopped by a scene of a St Andrew's cross and flogger. She and Matthew had once scened on this spot. She watched the rhythmic motion of the whip and felt herself getting warm between her thighs. The memories swamped her. Her heart started to beat faster. She couldn't breathe. She shouldn't be here. She turned on her feet and headed for the door but slammed straight into a solid wall of masculine chest. The scent of him engulfed her, warm, spicy--Matthew.

"Shh. Calm my sweetheart."

That voice.

Was she drunk? She pushed away from the familiar chest without even looking up to the face and began to run towards where she knew her boss was. But a booming voice echoed out silencing the whole club.

"Sonia. On your knees." Her body jerked, and she found herself dropping onto the floor. "You will stay there until I tell you to get up."

She shut her eyes trying to block out everything, but she could still feel the heat of everyone's glare upon her.

"Sonia." James' voice permeated her brain. "I need you to open your eyes and look in front of you."

She opened one eye and saw the kind and reassuring face of her boss. Everybody else faded into the background but her boss.

"He is gone. He left me to die."

"You know that isn't true."

"How can I know anything?"

"Here in this place, we work our differences out differently."

"What do you mean?"

"Your Master did not protect you as he should. He did not respect you as he should. You have the right to punish him."

"Punish him."

"Here, on the club floor."

"You're talking in riddles." She was so confused; she was a Sub; she didn't punish her Master did she?

"Sonia."

Matthew, her Matthew. He was alive, and he was here. He smiled at her, but it was a tentative one. He was nervous. He still had his arm in a sling, and he looked tired, but he was clean-shaven and seemed to bear little ill effects of the torture he suffered. Inside her, somewhere a burst of anger exploded, she had been stabbed, and he had run away like a coward. Jumping to her feet, she launched herself at him and sent a hit direct into his jaw. He staggered a few steps back as she wiggled her hand to try to get the pain now throbbing through it away. Damn, that man and his strong jaw.

"Fuck, Fuck, Fuck."

"Some ice," James called out, and the bartender was there in mere moments with a cold compress. Matthew stood back while James applied it.

"I should hit you as well for setting me up."

"Matthew will accept any punishment you chose to give him. I believe he once gave you a count of ten on this very floor for disobedience."

"He needs more than ten." She huffed.

"Then give it to him. Give him as many as you want. He will take it to prove he was a complete idiot. He wants to earn back your trust by placing himself in your hands."

She looked over to where Matthew stood to rub his jaw.

"I made the biggest mistake of my life running away. I broke the faith you had in me. This is the only way I think I can win it back."

"I don't know if I want you in my life anymore. Did you even care if I was still alive?"

"I received constant updates, but I became a chicken."

"Why now?"

"Because I realised the woman I was mourning for wasn't the one that was dead."

She swallowed. His words hitting her hard.

"Twenty."

"Twenty. What whip?"

She didn't know. She let Matthew choose them, generally. Whips were kind of his thing. Their thing.

"I suggest this one." James handed her one from Matthew's bag. "It is lightweight for you to swing, so it does not injure your stomach. It will still punish him though."

"He can't go on the cross with his arm."

"The bench is free."

The sea of people watching them parted and lined the way to the bench. Matthew had already started walking there.

"Wait. Your shoulder. I can't do this."

"I trust you to aim where you will not hurt me." He was back at her side and had taken her hand.

"Amber." She said the word and then clasped her hands over her mouth. She was trusting him again. James stepped away and bowed his head reverently.

"Why?"

"I don't want to hurt you." It was the most honest answer she could ever give. "I know what it is like to hurt, and I don't want to do that to you." A tear fell from her eye. Matthew looked around and she saw James motion to a side room.

"Come with me."

She took his hand and followed him into the small room. It was the one in which he had taken her virginity. Her heart constricted as the memories of that night flooded back.

"I still feel the moment you gave yourself to me every time I walk in this room."

"Don't."

"I'm sorry."

"For the comment? Or for running away?"

"Both. I have no excuse for what I did. I was a coward. I thought I'd failed you. I gave you my word I would always protect you, and when I saw you go down, I lost it."

"You should know better than that. A knife wound won't stop me."

"I was a complete fool."

"Yes, you were. Are coming back?"

"If you'll have me. James is pretty pissed off as well. I'm thinking you may be my boss now."

"I like the sound of that."

"Do you ever think you can forgive me?" Matthew fell to his knees before her. He looked so lost. He'd made a mistake, and he was grovelling for her forgiveness. Her tears were flowing freely now. He had let the darkness win at first, but then, in the end, he had controlled it and come back to her. She wasn't going to let her own darkness fester inside her. Matthew was her life; he was her future.

"Kiss me." The words left her mouth as the weight of the last few weeks flowed with them. She was free. His lips didn't hesitate to press against hers, and she was home.

He groaned. "I've missed that taste. It's uniquely you."

"Matthew."

"Yes, sweetheart."

"Make love to me."

"How is your stab wound?"

"Healing. Yours?"

"We might need to be a bit gentle on my arm. They had to pin it together."

"Ouch."

"Enough talk, Miss Anderson, more removal of your clothes please."

Within seconds she was naked. Him close behind her. His lips were at her body, remarking every inch. He kissed over the knife wound.

"Another scar." She sounded downbeat.

"Another mark for me to worship as a part of you." He kissed her wound again before going higher to her breasts. His tongue swirling around the tips as they peaked to hard nubs. She lay back on the bed as he worshipped every inch of her. She had missed his touch so much. He completed her. They didn't speak, he just slid inside her. Home. He was home.

Their eyes met. She held him in her gaze, and he thrust gently.

"I can't promise you marriage and children. I'm still so scared of that."

"I don't need them. I just need you and your love."

"You have that forever."

The heat started to build inside her.

"I love you."

"I love you too."

The first wave of her orgasm hit her. She couldn't take her eyes of Matthew. The shaking of her body matched his when he let out an elongated groan of pleasure, and she felt him flood her insides with his seed.

Home.

The word just kept reverberating around in her head.

"May I take you home Miss Anderson?" Matthew pulled

out of her, she whimpered at the loss of his warmth. She wanted him back inside her for at least a week before she would allow him out of her bed. James had better not plan on needing them for a while.

"You may Mr Sawyer, but first." A wicked grin spread across her face. "I do believe you owe me a count of twenty."

Marie and Callum's Wedding

Sonia looked around at everyone as they all watched Sally Bridgewater. What had their little group done to anger this woman? She was becoming a thorn in their sides. This time, however, she wasn't going to get a rise out of them.

"She wasn't just known as Mrs Carter. She was also known as Mrs Durand, Matthew's wife, or should I say, Matthias Durand." Miss Bridgewater continued her diatribe. The intrepid reporter thought that she was pushing her buttons.

"I believe a lot of that is classified information, Miss Bridgewater." Matthew stepped forward. He had his serious look on his face. He was ready to destroy the woman. Sonia was instantly back at his side. She linked her arm with his.

"Your lawyers cleared this story?"

"It was from a reliable source."

"A reliable source that has been playing you." She gave a smug smile.

"Pardon." The reporter didn't look so confident of herself now.

Sonia pointed to the part which stated that Jennifer Durand or Beth Parks had died in an explosion at the La Font mansion. The woman had no idea.

"Your source has given you misleading information. Either they don't know the full story, or they are wanting you to get sued for publishing misleading information."

"I don't understand." Sally flustered under the gaze of the wedding party.

"Matthew never killed his wife, she faked her own death."

All eyes went to Matthew, and he nodded his agreement.

"I thought for a long while it was my fault she died, but alas, I'm the innocent party. She was working for the other side."

"You are making it all up to make yourself look better. You sent her into that building. You knew she wasn't coming back out."

"I watched a woman I believed to be my wife walk into that building. What came out the other side was a monster." Matthew wrapped his arm around Sonia's waist.

"And if you publish that story you will be posting information on a top secret MI5 mission. I believe that even you are aware of the implications of that for anyone still working undercover. I don't think your editor will be impressed. I see the headlines now. 'Reporter responsible for hundreds of women being sold into slavery; all because of some personal vendetta.' You will never work again."

"Not with a formal complaint about harassment against my wife on your record as well." James stepped forward, Amy at his side.

"Publish away, Miss Bridgewater. As you can see I have no secrets from my girlfriend or my boss, so your story will do little to harm me. I care not for what the public think. I didn't go into MI5 for that. I saved people during my time there. Yes, there may have been sacrifices, but people survived because of me. That is all that matters."

Without a word, Miss Bridgewater turned on her heels and stomped off.

"I'm proud of you." Sonia stood up on her toes to kiss Matthew.

"People will always try to spoil love," Callum spoke this time, he had Marie in his arms and was kissing her.

"Yes, it's just jealousy on their part. I think Miss Bridgewater needs to get seriously laid and soon." Amy was kissing James in between all her words.

"Talking about getting laid, I think it is about time I escorted my wife to the bedroom." Callum patted Marie on the backside.

"Hey, not in front of my boss." Marie scolded her lover.

"I think your boss is having similar ideas for his wife." Sonia looked over to Amy and James. James was well on his way to getting his hands under Amy's long dress

"We've got no child for the night. We are going to make the most of it. Besides we want to make another one." Amy smiled.

"Amy, beautiful, they don't need those details."

Both couples disappeared to their respective rooms.

"Do you want another drink?" Matthew took hold of her hand and started to lead her back to the bar.

"I'd rather something else?"

"Something else?"

She pulled on his hand till it rested on the cleft between her thighs.

"Thank God for that. I thought you'd want me to dance till gone midnight. I've wanted you out of that dress all day." Matthew scooped her up into his arms and carried her at a rapid speed towards their bedroom. She couldn't stop laughing.

"Matthew, put me down. I need to tell you something."

"What." He did as she asked and searched her face for signs of anything being wrong. "What is the matter?"

She took his hand again, but this time she placed it on her stomach.

"I did a test this morning. I was late."

"Late for what?" She chuckled. For such a smart man he looked thoroughly confused.

"I'm pregnant."

"Pregnant?"

"Yes."

He went silent.

"How do you feel?"

"I feel fine. I need to pee a lot, but it's still early days. I'd like to see a doctor soon, though. I want to check everything to give me peace of mind."

"I'll get one arranged for tomorrow."

"Matthew."

"Yes."

"Are you alright?"

"You're pregnant."

"Are you angry?"

"Angry? Why would I be mad?"

He dropped to his knees in front of her and started to roll the hem of her dress up so that her stomach was exposed. "I'm taking in the emotion of the moment."

"What does that mean?"

He kissed her belly.

"You have a part of both of us growing inside you. I thought after everything with Beth I never wanted children. I couldn't look after my wife let alone myself, but right now, right now, my life is complete. You are going to have to cope with me being more protective than James was with Amy, but you are pregnant with my kid. I'm ecstatic." He was quickly onto his feet and twirling her around in the air. "I'm going to be a daddy."

"Put me down." She squirmed.

He instantly lowered her to her feet.

"Did I hurt you?"

"No. I'd just rather you make love to me as opposed to swinging me around the room."

"Isn't that the same thing?" He sniggered.

"Dork."

"You're a dork. Now get that sweet little arse on the bed, Miss Anderson, it's time for me to put myself back home."

Sally Bridgewater

"Well, that was quite a show." The slow rhythmic clap alerted her to his presence.

"You set me up." Sally Bridgewater turned venomously on the man in front of her.

"All part of the plan."

"And when are you going to tell me what your goal is?"

"Soon. Real soon but for now, I think you've earned what you wanted."

"What I wanted?"

"A chance at the man that destroyed your life." She rubbed her hands together in glee. "I want you to fly to Los Angeles. All expenses paid of course. There is someone there that I 'd like you to meet."

"Who is she?"

"I didn't say it was a she."

"If it involves that man it will be a she. It's always she and normally not just one."

"Boy, we do have it bad for him."

"I hate his fucking guts and can't wait to destroy him."

"Tut, tut, tut, that bad in bed was he?"

She curled her lip.

"We both know I'm the best fuck you ever had."

"Yeah, you were, until you broke my jaw."

"An accident." He stroked her hand down his cheek.

"One I won't forget." He roughly grasped her breast and started to knead it. His hard cock pressed against her thigh. What was it about the bad boys she couldn't resist?

"How about I take it a little more gently this time." His hand moved from her breast down to her pussy. She was gone. He would have her again tonight. And tomorrow she would fly to Los Angeles. Her prey was in sight. He maybe a Hawk in his native roots but Grayson Moore was a pesky fly she was going to squash.

THE END

The story continues in July 2017 in Controlling Heritage – Grayson Moore and Sophie North's story.

Previous Books in the Control Series

Surrendered Control, The Control Series, Book 1:
Amazon US http://amzn.to/2gDAgtG
Amazon UK http://amzn.to/2gGShn5
Goodreads http://bit.ly/2fOdQEK

Divided Control, The Control Series, Book 2:
Amazon US http://amzn.to/2gutKT7
Amazon UK http://amzn.to/2gDqV58
Goodreads http://bit.ly/2gdtMhv

Misguided Control, The Control Series, Book 3:
AmazonUK: http://amzn.to/2lxiqM0
Amazon US: http://amzn.to/2lxojca
Goodreads: http://bit.ly/2rEaxa5

Dear Reader,

I hope you enjoyed this book. I'd love it if you could post a review about it on Amazon and Goodreads. Getting reviews for my books is such a thrill as it allows me to see what readers enjoy or even, dislike about what I write. It's all good for me to learn. Perhaps you could mention which is your favourite character and what parts you like best. You could also say which character you're looking forward to reading more about in a new book.

If you've spotted a typo, email me at
anna1000edwards@gmail.com.

I look forward to hearing from you.

Anna Edwards

PS – Read on for a preview of my new series!

Coming in June 2017 a new series from international author Anna Edwards, The Glacial Blood Series, a paranormal romance series.

The barren desert wasteland with its hues of gold, orange and red sped passed the car window. The rock formations a testament to the years of erosion beaten down upon them by force greater than even he could understand, and as a shape-shifting snow leopard, Brayden Dillion understood a lot about the ways of Mother Nature. The brand new Ford Mustang he drove had been a gift from his Alpha in recognition for a job done well. As was the break from duties. Although why his mother had to live just outside Death Valley in Furnace Creek was beyond him. You really couldn't get a hotter place on Earth and considering he spent most of his time exploring the snow-capped peaks of The Glacial national park he already had the air-con turned right up. She'd told him that it was because of his father, he'd always lived in the snow so when he died, she decided to get some sun for once. And she hadn't looked back. He pulled his Mustang up outside the café with a roar of the high powered engine. The disapproving looks from the locals soon vanished when he climbed out of the car. His long, muscular legs topped with a stocky body and a height of almost six foot five silenced any potential disagreement. He purred to himself in contentment, but that was quickly lost when the heat of the midday sun hit him. He was not designed for this weather, he had all the usual snow leopard attributes, thick black hair with smoky grey flecks, small ears and big feet that helped with balance. He was pale in colour because he very rarely spent time sunbathing like the lions and tigers in his pack. Dusk or dawn was when he was the most active. He made quick steps towards the café and into the air-conditioned building. Looking around he didn't see his mother but only a new faced waitress who wore the cafes' uniform of a barely there skirt and a tank top as a second skin. She was pretty, in a timid sort of way. Every time someone came near her she flinched, and he could smell her fear. Well, he assumed it was her fear as his judgement was slightly clouded by the fact that he needed a drink, preferably ice cold and dumped over his head. She approached the seat he had taken near the counter.

"Hi, welcome to the 'Last Stop'. I'm Selene, and I'll be your waitress today. You look at little hot, can I get you an ice water to start with? It sure is a hot one out there today." Any sign of her nerves had disappeared and was replaced with a business like smiles.

"Yes please, lots of ice. In fact, just bring me a big bowl of ice."

She laughed at his comment. Her tiny nose crinkling up and dimples appearing in her cheeks.

"Let me guess." She took a step back and looked him up and down. "Well the fact you seem like you're melting, I take it you're not a southerner. The lack of a tan confirms that but I can't quite place the accent?"

"Montana."

"No wonder you're hot. I'll bring you ice cream as well." She spun around in her little ballet pumps and started to stride off. Something stopped her though. She turned back and took another long look at him.

"Brayden?"

ABOUT ANNA EDWARDS

Anna Edwards is a British Author that has a love of travelling and developing plot lines for stories. She has spent that last two years learning the skills of writing after being an Accountant since the age of 21. As well as Roleplaying on twitter, she can also be found writing poetry on twitter under the account, Jane @harmoniccascade.

Her debut novel, Surrendered Control was released in November 2016 and has received fantastic feedback on the drama of story.

In her writing she loves to combine her love for romantic and erotic novels with her passion for travel to give an international feel to her novels. Yorkshire, she travelled to with friends recently and was captured by the beauty of it and the kindness of the locals.

For her tenth wedding anniversary, she travelled to The Wynn with her husband. While they didn't exactly hit the high rollers room they enjoyed the experience of being treated like royalty.

CONNECT WITH ANNA EDWARDS

www.AuthorAnnaEdwards.com

Facebook, Author Page: AnnaEdwardsWriter

Facebook, Friend: TheAuthorAnnaEdwards

Twitter: @Anna__Edwards

Instagram: authorannaedwards

Pinterest: anna1000edwards

Goodreads: anna__edwards

Email: anna1000edwards@gmail.com

Printed in Great Britain
by Amazon